Darkness Falls

When Frank and Joe win a trip to Hawaii as part of a prestigious science prize, they think the most excitement they'll get is watching the once-in-a-lifetime total solar eclipse. But their scientific research soon takes a back seat as the researcher they came to see is murdered right outside the observatory. It seems that the world of science isn't as clinical as the brothers had first imagined, but is riddled with petty jealousies, greed and hatred. Hatred strong enough that it can even lead to murder.

Titles in *THE HARDY BOYS*™ Pocket Books series:

HARDY BOYS™

Darkness Falls

POCKET BOOKS

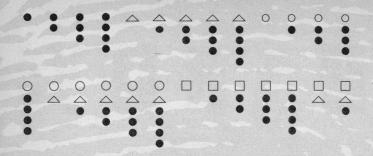

This is no ordinary book! It holds the key to *a secret Hardy Boys mystery* and the chance to win an awesome prize!

Printed somewhere in each book in the new Hardy Boys series is a case code. Collect every code and by January 2000 you will have eleven. The case codes make up a secret message - only you can crack it!

When *Sabotage at Sea* is published in January 2000 you will find an entry form and all the competition details printed inside the book. Good luck!

POCKET
BOOKS

An imprint of Simon & Schuster UK Ltd
Africa House, 64-78 Kingsway
London WC2B 6AH

Copyright © 1999 by Viacom International Inc.
All rights reserved.
Illustrations by Colin Howard Copyright © Viacom International Inc.
POCKET BOOKS and colophon are registered
trademarks of Simon & Schuster
A CIP catalogue record for this book is
available from the British Library

ISBN 0 671 02896 0

1 3 5 7 9 10 8 6 4 2

Printed by Caledonian International Book Manufacturing, Glasgow

This book was originally published in Great Britain
as an ARCHWAY PAPERBACK number 89

Chapter

1

"AND NOW, approaching the podium to receive his Ebersol Foundation Science Award, is Mr. Frank Hardy!" Joe Hardy pretended to hold a microphone to his mouth as he roared like an overexcited TV announcer. Joe's brother Frank didn't react, but continued to stride toward the full-length mirror on his bedroom door and knot his tie.

"The girls in the audience are swooning, ladies and gentlemen!" Joe continued. "The very sight of the young genius is more than they can take!"

Sitting on the bed, Biff Hooper and Chet Morton, two of the Hardys' oldest friends, grinned at Joe. Biff leaned back on his powerful arms to relax and enjoy the show while Chet leaned forward to peel off the wrapper from his fourth candy bar.

"You look good in a suit, Frank," Biff said. "I didn't even know you owned one."

"But wait!" Joe cried, stepping between Frank and the mirror. "What's this flurry of excitement in the back of the hall? Why, it's Frank's brother, Joe Hardy, co-winner of the prize! Joe's dazzling good looks have completely eclipsed those of his older—though not wiser—brother. The crowd is going absolutely wild!" Joe spun around to gaze into the mirror, obviously admiring himself.

Biff and Chet laughed as Frank elbowed Joe away. "Excuse me," Frank said with a wry grin, "but don't you have some packing to do?"

"It's obvious that Joe got the lion's share of good looks in the Hardy family, folks," Joe shot back in his TV voice. He ran a hand over his brother's brown hair, messing it up totally. "Comb your hair, Frank. It's a disaster."

Frank took out a comb and carefully put his hair back in place. "Get the talking out of your system now, Joe, because when it's time to speak to the press, I'll do the talking. I did most of the work on the project, so it's only fair."

Joe turned to face Chet and Biff. "You don't

believe that, do you? I'm the brilliant one, right?"

"No comment," Chet said around a mouthful of caramel and chocolate.

"Double no comment," Biff echoed. "Hey, when did you guys become scientists, anyway? I knew you were detectives, but scientists?"

"It just happened," Frank confessed. "We'd been tinkering with a new kind of infrared film for taking pictures at night—"

"And then *I* figured out a way to treat the film to make a better image," Joe interrupted.

Frank yawned and picked a piece of lint off the sleeve of his new suit. "But," he said, "who suggested that we try it out on a night sky? If we hadn't taken shots of the stars and entered them in the state science fair, Dr. Ebersol would never have seen our new film and invited us to go to Hawaii with him to help photograph the solar eclipse."

Fenton Hardy, Frank and Joe's detective father, had stepped into the doorway in time to hear what Frank said. "It's a good thing I taught you boys to be modest," he remarked, putting an arm around Frank's shoulders. "It's almost six-thirty, and your mother and aunt Gertrude are already on their way to the award ceremony. If you keep arguing about who deserves the credit, we'll miss it."

3

"I guess you guys inherited your brains from your dad," Chet said, getting up off the bed.

Biff stood up, too, and soon all of them had piled into Mr. Hardy's sedan, driving to the state university campus on the edge of Bayport.

"I don't know what I'm more excited about," Frank confessed, "the award or the trip to Hawaii that goes along with it."

"Are you kidding?" Joe teased. "Have you forgotten the waves, the beaches, the beautiful girls?"

"Have you forgotten that we nearly got ourselves killed there?" Frank replied, reminding his brother of their problems the last time they'd been in Hawaii.

"That was different," Joe said. "We were on a case, chasing down a major crime boss."

"Have you guys ever noticed," Chet said, "that wherever you go, cases follow you?"

"Well, it's not going to happen this time," Fenton Hardy said. "There's not much room for criminal mischief when you're at the top of an extinct volcano, surrounded by scientists who are studying the longest solar eclipse of the century."

"You never know with Frank and Joe," Biff insisted.

Frank was barely listening. His mind had drifted back to the award ceremony. He could hardly believe that they were about to meet Dr. James Ebersol—the man who had done more than any single person to make astronomy a household word. At the height of his fame, five years earlier, Dr. Ebersol had had three books on the best-seller list at the same time. One was about black holes, another was about space travel, and the third was about other life forms in the galaxy. His weekly TV show, "The Universe Explained," had been on for years. Going to Hawaii with him and his research team was the opportunity of a lifetime.

"Dreaming of sun and surf, Frank?" Chet asked, breaking into Frank's reverie.

"More like sun and stars," Frank said. "We've been joking about it, but the truth is, I'm still in shock. We may actually help discover the first new planet in our solar system in a hundred years!"

"Does Ebersol really believe there's another planet out there?" Biff asked dubiously. "Wouldn't it have been discovered by now?"

"That's just the thing," Joe broke in. "Until recently, there was no way to prove it. According to Ebersol, this planet—if it ever existed—was blown to bits billions of years ago, and it's only with advanced infrared photography that the Ebersol team may be able to capture the remaining debris on film. That's why when he heard about our infrared film project winning first place at the science fair, Ebersol asked us to come along."

When they arrived at the campus, Fenton Hardy parked behind the ultramodern building that was the home of the school's astronomy department. They entered through a rear door and found themselves in a long corridor. "We're looking for Room one-oh-nine," Fenton reminded the boys.

The room, just a few yards away, was a fairly large lecture hall with a dais and podium, and curved, arena-style seating. The front row had a few reporters loading film in their cameras and making notes. Laura Hardy, Frank and Joe's mother, sat in the fifth row with the boys' aunt Gertrude. When the two women saw the Hardys appear in the doorway, they smiled proudly and waved.

"I hope you're our winners," a plump young woman in a plaid dress said, approaching the group. "I'm P. J. O'Malley of the Ebersol Foundation. I'm looking for Joe and Frank Hardy."

"These guys, right here," Chet said, proudly patting each of his friends on the shoulder.

"It's nice to meet you," she said with a smile. "Unfortunately, Mr. De La Rosa, the manager of the foundation, couldn't be here to welcome you in person, but he asked me to extend his sincere congratulations. He'll be joining you in Hawaii the night after the eclipse, so you'll meet him then."

"Good luck, fellas," Fenton said, leaving with Chet and Biff to join his wife. "We'll be watching."

"Your seats are the last two on the right," P.J. told Frank and Joe, pointing to the dais.

"Thanks." Frank felt a rush as a large set of spotlights came on. A local TV news crew was setting up to film the ceremony.

Frank and Joe had just taken their places when a tall man with piercing blue eyes and a charismatic manner strode up to them. With him was a woman in her late twenties with large brown eyes and flowing auburn hair. "You must be Joe Hardy," the man said, brushing back his long mane of gray hair and offering his hand. "I'm Jim Ebersol. We spoke on the phone."

"Yes, sir. I recognize you," Frank said, standing up. "But I'm Frank. This is Joe."

"Pleasure to meet you both," Ebersol said, shaking Frank's hand, then Joe's. "I'm looking forward to having you on our expedition. Oh, by the way, this is my wife."

"My name is Michele," she said with a smile almost as dazzling as her husband's. "Your photographs were spectacular. Congratulations!" Michele's peasant-style dress with embroidered flowers emphasized her youthful appearance. She had to be at least fifteen years younger than her husband, Frank thought.

"Michele fancies herself an expert in infrared," Dr. Ebersol said, putting an arm around her shoulders and giving her a little squeeze. "Her master's thesis was on it. Wasn't it, dear?"

"Have you forgotten already?" his wife protested with a smile, though Frank noticed a slight edge to her voice.

"Where's Everett?" Ebersol asked, peering out over the assembly. "I want to introduce him, too."

"Right here, sir," said a man who'd been sitting quietly on the other side of the dais, his nose buried in a scientific journal. He was pale, with thinning blond hair and dark-rimmed glasses. Frank guessed he was about thirty.

"Come over and meet the Hardy brothers!" Ebersol told him. "Boys, this is my longtime assistant, Everett MacLaughlin, who'll be with us in Hawaii. Some day, I predict he'll make quite a name for himself with his own discoveries."

"You're very kind, sir," the assistant said, acting uncomfortable with the praise. He gave the Hardys a terse smile and returned to his seat.

"Excuse me, Dr. Ebersol," P.J. said, tapping

him on the shoulder. "If we're going to get a clip on the evening news, we have to get started."

Frank gazed out at the auditorium, which was nearly filled now. A woman in a navy blue suit rose from her seat and approached the podium. Frank recognized her as Hillary Burns, the president of the university.

"Tonight," Ms. Burns began, "we're privileged to have a great scientist with us. He is perhaps the best-known astrophysicist since Galileo, thanks to the power of the media and the brilliance of his discoveries. Please give a warm welcome to the Great Explainer, Dr. James Ebersol!"

Everyone rose and applauded as Dr. Ebersol exchanged places with Dr. Burns. Frank's hands stung from clapping as he sat back down to listen.

"Thank you," Ebersol began. "It's an honor to be at this university, which was so supportive of my work while I was here and continues to support me at the Ebersol Foundation. I'm extremely proud to be able to give something back tonight—an Ebersol Foundation grant to establish a new library of astronomy and astrophysics." This announcement was met with more enthusiastic applause.

"I'd like at this time to acknowledge the two young men seated up here with me. Frank and

Joe Hardy discovered an important component of accurate infrared film development and used this film to shoot the night sky and stars. The Ebersol Foundation would like to honor them and their achievement tonight with the Ebersol Science Award. Frank? Joe?"

Frank flushed as flashes went off and he and Joe rose to accept their bronze plaque.

"Thanks very much, Dr. Ebersol," Frank managed to say, taking the plaque. The bright lights suddenly felt intensely hot and blinding to him.

"My brother and I would also like to thank our parents and the people at the university photography lab who let us use their equipment," Joe said as smoothly as a professional speaker. Frank was impressed. During another small burst of applause, the brothers shook Dr. Ebersol's hand and returned to their seats.

"Search for the stars," Dr. Ebersol continued, his voice softening dramatically as he repeated the phrase slowly. "Search for the stars—it's almost an unwritten commandment, isn't it? And it began the moment our ancestors first raised their eyes from their caves to the complex, starry night sky. It's a pursuit that has motivated me since I can remember. And now I stand on the brink of what may be my greatest discovery—the Exploded Planet."

Staring out into the audience, Frank saw that

everyone seemed enthralled by Ebersol's dramatic exposition.

"A quest of this magnitude takes a lot of effort, and a lot of resources, and I'd like to thank my supporters for making the search possible," the scientist continued. "It has long been my belief that to be complete humans beings, we must always feel the awe our ancestors felt as they studied the stars. Yes, my friends, our true human destiny—to discover—can only be fulfilled when we search for the stars!"

There was a moment of silence as Dr. Ebersol's inspiring words faded. Then, a smattering of applause began, followed immediately by enthusiastic clapping.

Acknowledging the acclaim with a modest smile. Dr. Ebersol added, "Now I'll be happy to take questions from the press. I'm sure you're all curious about the coming eclipse. You, there," he said, pointing to a reporter waving her pencil in the air.

"Could you explain your 'exploded planet' theory for us, sir?" she asked. "And also, what do you hope to achieve during the coming eclipse?"

"Certainly," Dr. Ebersol said warmly. "My theory holds that at the birth of our solar system, there were more than nine planets. But one of them, or possibly even two, were pulled into the sun's gravitational force, where they blew apart.

"My theory could only be proven by finding a ring of cosmic rubble around the sun," he went on. "Now, why have we never spotted this ring? Simply because the sun is too bright. But with the new infrared detectors developed by my team, Michele Ebersol and Everett MacLaughlin, and with the two young Hardys, my guess is that we'll be able to spot the rings during the eclipse."

"But, Doctor," another reporter said, "we've had eclipses before. What makes this one special?"

"This eclipse is far and away the longest in our lifetime," Ebersol replied. "Imagine! The sun's rays will be totally obliterated for a full seven minutes! If I may add a small historical footnote—I find it ironic that in ancient times a solar eclipse was considered an evil omen, foretelling the death of kings. Now we view an eclipse as a scientific opportunity. Our perspective has certainly changed, hasn't it?"

The science editor of the local TV station rose and waved his hand. "Where will you be taking the photographs, Doctor?" he shouted.

"I've chosen the Mauna Kea Observatory in Hawaii for my experiment," Ebersol replied. "It's extremely fortunate that the eclipse will take place over one of the greatest astronomical research facilities in the world. And the mountain's elevation—over thirteen thousand feet, above half of the earth's atmosphere—reduces interference from dust and water vapor. If there are no more questions, I want to thank you all for coming, and wish us luck."

Ebersol waved to the crowd, then turned back to the row of chairs behind him. Before the applause could begin, a voice shouted out from the back of the auditorium.

"Dr. Ebersol! Tim Wheeler of *Astronomy Today*. Just one quick question. Which is more important to you, Doctor—finding this destroyed planet, or getting your next book onto the best-seller lists?"

Frank watched as Ebersol's back stiffened. Clenching his fists, the Great Explainer made his way back to the metal podium to answer the impudent question. He grabbed the microphone in one hand.

As he did so, there was a sudden sizzling sound, and a shower of sparks flew out from the mike. Ebersol screamed in agony, and several others in the audience screamed, too.

Frank couldn't believe it—Dr. Ebersol was being electrocuted right in front of their eyes!

Chapter

2

FRANK SPRANG toward the podium, but Joe was quicker. Knowing that if he touched Ebersol with his feet on the ground, he, too, would be electrocuted, Joe leaped high with both feet, kicking Ebersol free of the mike. The two toppled to the floor.

There was pandemonium in the hall as the group on stage crowded around. Frank checked Ebersol's pulse. "Get an ambulance!" Frank shouted. Then, as Joe got up, he asked, "Are you okay?"

"I think so," Joe said, rubbing his back.

Frank bent down and loosened Ebersol's tie; the great man's eyes opened. "Are you all right, sir?" he asked. Ebersol nodded, but Frank could tell he was woozy. Just then Michele knelt by her husband's side. "Jim, darling," she whispered.

Frank stepped back to make room for her and gestured for Joe to come with him. The two brothers went straight to the podium to check the wiring visually. "Don't touch anything," Frank warned. "We'll have to make sure the circuit breaker is off first."

P.J. came up to them. "You can touch it," she said. "I just shut it off." She bent over to check out the mike, too.

"Who turned on the mike?" Frank asked as Joe traced the wiring.

"It was all set up when we arrived," said the woman. "The university keeps it ready."

"Hmmm," Joe said, holding a wire in his hands. "Here's the problem. This wire's been stripped down." He showed them the spot where the insulation had been worn away.

"Do you think it was cut deliberately?" Frank asked, examining it.

Joe frowned. "If it *was* deliberate, somebody took great care to make it look natural."

"But why would anyone want to electrocute Dr. Ebersol?" P.J. asked. "Accidents do happen, after all."

"I hope you're right," said Joe. "All the same, Frank, we'd better keep an eye on Ebersol from now on."

*   *   *

The next afternoon Joe and Frank boarded the plane to Hawaii. "No matter how many times I've flown, I still get excited," Joe admitted as he and Frank showed their passes to the crew.

"*You're* excited," Frank said, smiling. "Did you see how keyed up Mom was when she said goodbye? I think she's already planning the celebration party she'll throw when we get back."

Before they turned to the right into coach, they saw Dr. Ebersol and his wife, standing in first class, getting ready to sit. Fortunately, Ebersol had recovered from his shock, except for a bandage on one hand. "I'm bored already, and I can't even write!" Joe heard him complain. "Get me *The New York Times,* Michele."

When he turned and saw Frank and Joe, Ebersol transformed his grumpy expression into his familiar, brilliant smile. "It won't be long now, boys!" he said.

"Excuse me, I need to get by to get to the magazine rack," Michele said to Joe, who had stepped into first class. Joe noticed that she seemed tired and stressed.

"Hi, remember me?" Joe said. She glanced up at him and gave a little laugh.

"Sorry," she said with a sigh. "I'm not very together today. Jim's hand was bothering him last night and neither of us got any sleep."

The Hardys left to find their seats in coach.

Across the aisle from them, Everett Mac-Laughlin was gazing out the window, a serious expression on his face.

"Hey, there," Joe said, sliding into his seat.

The graduate assistant reacted as if he was startled. "Oh. Hi," he said. Quickly, he picked up a scientific journal on his lap and began reading.

The plane stopped in San Francisco, then landed in Honolulu, where the group changed planes for their flight to Kona Airport on the island of Hawaii—Big Island, as the locals called it. By the time they landed, the summer sun was setting over the ocean in an orange and pink blaze of glory.

As they got off the plane, Joe took a deep breath. Even at the airport, the evening breeze carried the scent of orchids.

"It's weird going back in time, isn't it?" Frank said, resetting his wristwatch. "Just think, in Hawaii they see the evening news in the morning."

Dr. Ebersol called Frank and Joe over to him. "Michele and I have to meet with some of the foundation's sponsors at the beach house we've rented," he told them. "Please help Everett unload the equipment. Then he'll take you to your hotel. I'll see you up at the observatory tomorrow morning, and we'll set up shop."

"You got it," Frank said cheerfully.

The Hardys and MacLaughlin stowed the gear in a rented van. Frank and Joe decided to rent a car of their own, in case there was time for exploring the island. They followed MacLaughlin's blue van in a shiny red convertible, past lava fields that looked like moonscapes in the growing twilight and on to the resort town of Kailua.

Their hotel was a budget one on the noisy main drag. Joe's eyes widened when he got a load of the surfboards for rent in the shop next door. "Let's make time for those before we leave here," he said to Frank, who nodded his agreement.

After unpacking, the boys knocked on MacLaughlin's door. "Join us for dinner?" Frank asked.

"I can't," the assistant answered nervously. "I'm going over the data, preparing for tomorrow."

"Okay," Frank said. "Maybe next time, then."

"Does that guy ever take a break?" Joe asked as they headed for the nearest restaurant.

Frank shook his head. "Maybe *he* should try surfing!"

Seated at a sidewalk café with a perfect view of the beach, Frank told the waiter, "We'll have two Hawaiian burgers with pineapple rings."

"Right," Joe agreed, shutting his menu. "I'll try anything once."

The waiter had just left when the Hardys were approached by a dark-haired man Frank guessed to be in his thirties. "You're the Hardys, aren't you?" he asked. "I'm Tim Wheeler of *Astronomy Today*. I was at the award ceremony last night. Congratulations."

Joe and Frank were surprised. "You're the one who asked Dr. Ebersol about being a publicity hound," Joe said, his eyes narrowing.

"Guilty," Wheeler admitted offhandedly.

"When did you get to Hawaii?" Joe asked, surprised to see the reporter. "I didn't see you on the plane."

"I took the red-eye," Wheeler said. When Joe seemed confused, he smiled. "That's what you call an overnight flight. I flew to Los Angeles last night and arrived in Honolulu this morning."

"But why did you come?" Frank asked.

"I'm writing the script for a documentary film about the eclipse," Wheeler explained.

When the waiter came with the Hardys' food, the reporter asked to join them and ordered a papaya smoothie.

"You're detectives, right? I've read about you in the Bayport *News*," Wheeler said. "Hey! Maybe you can figure out who tried to fry the Great Explainer last night."

"Is that what you think happened?" Frank asked, scrutinizing the reporter.

Wheeler winced and shook his head. "Anything's possible," he replied. "You've got to admit, Jim Ebersol is not particularly well-liked—not by anyone who knows him, that is."

"What makes you say that?" Frank asked. "I thought he was widely respected."

"Respect is one thing," Wheeler said. "Being liked is another."

"Well, Ebersol would never have gotten that electric shock if you hadn't provoked him to come back to the podium," Joe said accusingly.

"Whoa," said Wheeler, holding up both hands. "I don't go around hot-wiring mikes!"

"But you don't like Ebersol," Joe said, playing it straight. "Why not?"

Wheeler scowled. "I think the guy is a bombastic old windbag. But that doesn't mean I'd *hurt* him."

"Why do you feel that way about him?" Frank asked.

Wheeler let out a sigh. "I guess it won't hurt to tell you," he said. "I was once engaged to the sweetest, prettiest astronomy student this side of M.I.T.—Michele Mendez, now Michele Ebersol."

"What happened?" Joe asked softly.

Wheeler shook his head and took a sip of the smoothie the waiter had placed in front of him.

"Oh, it's a typical story," he said, making light of what he was saying. "Two young astronomy students fall in love, until an established genius shows up and sweeps one of them off her feet. When Ebersol fell for Michele, there was no way I could compete with his money, his power, or his fame. Before I knew it, she had given me back my ring."

"But you're a reporter, not an astronomer," Joe pointed out, confused.

"Ebersol iced me out of the astronomy department, so I transferred to journalism and tried science writing," Wheeler said with a sigh. "I've done okay, but I still can't forgive him for stealing Michele. It was six years ago, but it feels like yesterday."

"That's sad," Joe said quietly.

"And it's a long time to be carrying a torch for someone," Frank added.

"You know, I'd make myself forget her in a minute if I thought she was happy," Wheeler said thoughtfully. "But when I see her, well— the sparkle's missing from her eyes." Wheeler shook his head, then stood up. "I think I'll get some sleep. Tomorrow's a big day. See you." After putting money on the table, he waved and walked away.

"Well, he sure gave us something to think about," Joe said.

"I liked him," Frank said. "I can't blame him

for not liking Ebersol. If he stole my girl and iced me out—"

"But, Frank, do you think—?"

"That Wheeler stripped that wire to hurt him?" Frank finished for him. "I guess it's possible. But if he had, why would he tell us about his past history?"

"Maybe he's just weird," Joe said, watching the reporter wander away. "In any case, we should keep an eye on him."

The next morning the Hardys hooked up with Everett MacLaughlin after breakfast and began the drive up the coast to Saddle Road, which crossed the island to the extinct Mauna Kea, with its observatory.

"Funny—I don't feel any jet lag," Frank said.

"It's probably because you're so excited about the eclipse," Joe suggested. "I know I am. How about you, Mr. MacLaughlin? Are you excited?"

"Me?" the assistant asked, keeping his eyes on the road as he drove. "I suppose I'm experiencing a fair degree of excitement." Frank couldn't help thinking that MacLaughlin seemed uncomfortable or unused to any attention. The perfect image of a science nerd, he thought.

In a matter of minutes they had driven from the island's dry western coast, through lush jungle vegetation near Mauna Kea, and then up into scrub and grassland at a higher elevation. The wind howled as they passed through the thick layer of fog that blanketed the mountains a thousand feet below their summits. They found the turnoff to the observatory and zigzagged up hairpin turns, emerging from the clouds to see the majestic peak of Mauna Kea, with the domed observatory a hundred feet or so below it.

The huge parking lot was filled with scientists and their assistants unloading equipment. A sign read Observatory Closed to General Public Day of Eclipse. Research Teams Proceed to Assigned Viewing Spaces.

"Wow," Joe said, letting out a whistle. "This place is intense."

"And busy. Have you ever been here before, Mr. MacLaughlin?" Frank asked, hoping to draw the graduate assistant into conversation.

All he got was a quiet no.

Surrounding the observatory were several smaller buildings, equipped with tall antennae and radar dishes. There were also at least a dozen large trailers, along with an assortment of tents positioned all around the mountaintop.

Dr. Ebersol met them as they emerged from the van. "Good morning," he said brightly, ready for action. "You'll be setting up two tents this morning—one for me and the computers, and a silver aluminized, light-tight tent, for you, your cameras, and the infrared detectors. Come, I'll show you."

Ebersol led them to a spot about twenty-five yards away, where his wife stood next to a pile of silver aluminized tent pieces. Michele's hair was bound up in a bun on top of her head, but Frank noticed that even in her lab coat, she still looked great. She was definitely a woman two men might fight over, he thought to himself.

"The observatory has loaned us these tents," Ebersol said.

"Here are the instructions," Michele told them, handing a booklet to Everett. "The tents should be fairly easy to construct. Once they're up, you can load in the gear from the van."

"Aren't you going to stay to help?" Everett asked, sounding surprised.

Dr. Ebersol put his arm around his wife's shoulders. "Michele and I have to meet with the observatory scientists now. We'll check in with you after lunch, though."

After the Ebersols left, it took about an hour and a half for the Hardys and MacLaughlin to build the tents and connect all the instruments, cameras, and computers to the cable hookup from the observatory telescopes.

"What next?" Frank asked MacLaughlin when the last cable was connected.

The graduate assistant pursed his lips and

looked around the inside of the aluminized tent. "I think everything's under control," he said, sounding more cheerful than he had earlier. "You two can take a break for about an hour while I double-check the equipment."

"You're sure we can go?" Frank asked. The assistant didn't answer as he already had his back to them, tinkering with cable connections.

"Come on, Frank," Joe said. "Let's check out this scene."

They stepped out under the spectacularly bright Hawaiian sky, skirted the parking lot, and noticed several trails leading down the mountainside. Next to one, a paved path, they spotted Tim Wheeler talking to a young dark-haired man in a denim shirt.

"Hey, guys! What's up?" Wheeler called when he noticed them. "Are you working hard?"

"We were, but we're done for the moment," Frank explained.

"Me, too," Wheeler said cheerfully. "But my pal Jake and I just thought of a way to have some fun. Jake, this is Frank and Joe Hardy."

"Hi," the man said before he turned back to Tim. "You got it wrong, man. No way am I going to ride a bike down that road. I'm not *that* crazy."

Tim's eyes were twinkling mischievously.

"How about you, guys? Are you up for some excitement?"

"What kind of excitement?" Joe asked dubiously.

"There are a bunch of old bikes lying around," Wheeler said. "I guess the scientists up here use them to get around. I think it might be a blast to coast down the road all the way to Saddle Road. Want to try—kind of a race?"

Frank and Joe grinned at each other. The road, with its hairpin turns and thick fog, would be a real challenge on a bike. And Wheeler had dared them to a race. "You're on, mister!" Joe said, giving Wheeler a high five.

"Are you sure, Joe?" Frank said cautiously. "We have to be back in an hour."

"No problem," Wheeler said. "Jake'll drive his van down to Saddle Road and pick us up. It's only about four miles. Then we can load up the bikes and ride back up in style."

"Sounds good," Frank said. "Let's get started!"

A few minutes later the three were breezing down the steep road, frightened and thrilled at the same time. Wheeler was good but an amateur. The Hardys were experienced bike racers. Even on old clunkers, they were soon far ahead of him. When they plunged into the fog bank they finally had to hit the brakes because they were no longer able to see very far ahead.

All at once Joe heard the noise of a car engine behind them. He turned to check on it and saw that it was a van and the vehicle's headlights were close, and closing too fast. The van was directly behind Frank, not moving over to pass him.

"Pull over, Frank!" Joe shouted back over his shoulder to his brother. But the roar of the engine had gotten louder now and Frank hadn't heard. He must have thought the van was going around him, Joe thought. Joe had to turn forward right then to steady his bike.

On one side was the wall of solid rock. On the other, a sheer drop-off. And there wasn't enough room between for the van to pass now even if the driver wanted to.

In seconds it would have to push them right off the mountain!

Chapter

3

JOE FRANTICALLY searched for any way to escape as he skidded into a hairpin turn at breakneck speed. The van had to slow down to keep from skidding off the road, so the bikes sailed ahead, gaining a few seconds of precious time.

Once they were back on the straightaway, the van started gaining on them again. Joe knew it was only seconds before they were either run down or run off the cliff.

Then he saw their salvation. Up ahead and on the left, a small thicket of bushes covered a narrow gap in the mountainside wall. "There, Frank!" he shouted, pointing, and aimed his bike right at it. The bike hit the bushes and stopped dead, sending Joe hurtling through the air. His fall was cushioned by the bushes as the van roared by.

"Frank! Are you all right?" Joe shouted, checking to make sure he himself didn't have any broken bones.

"Ow! Ow!" came Frank's voice from behind him. "This bush is full of thorns!"

Joe almost laughed when he parted the bushes and found Frank, already on his feet, pulling thorns out of the seat of his pants. "Let me help," Joe said, yanking one out as his brother yelped in pain.

"What in the world did that guy in the van think he was doing?" Frank asked angrily. "We might have been killed!"

"Maybe that was the idea," Joe said. "Or am I being paranoid?"

"I don't know," Frank said. "Maybe his brakes just went bad or something. Why would anyone want to kill us, Joe?"

"No reason I can think of," Joe had to admit. "But then, I can't think of any reason to electrocute Ebersol, either."

Just then Tim Wheeler came to a stop beside them on the road. "Hey, you two," he called. "Are you all right? That guy was driving like a maniac!"

"No kidding," Joe agreed. "We were just discussing whether he was trying to kill us or not."

"Oh, I don't think so," Wheeler said, obviously shocked at the thought. "He swerved to get out of my way as he passed me. Maybe he just couldn't stop."

"Well, he didn't try to get out of *our* way," Joe said. "As a matter of fact, I think he gunned his engine when he got near us."

"Maybe he couldn't see you in the fog," Wheeler suggested.

"Maybe," Joe said tersely. "Anyway, we'd better get back and tell somebody about this. We might be able to trace the van. No one got a license number, right?"

"No," Frank said. "It was much too foggy, but I saw the van as it moved out of the fog. It was steel gray with a bubble top. Somebody at the observatory ought to know it."

"Jake should be going by any minute now," Wheeler said. "But he won't be able to stop on this road. We'll have to go down to Saddle Road and wait for him there. Do you think your bikes will make it?" Frank and Joe nodded.

An hour later all three were back at the observatory. The gray van with the bubble turned out to belong to a visiting research team from Japan. They had left the keys in the ignition and were quite upset that someone had used it for a joy ride and then abandoned it on Saddle Road.

"So much for the bad brakes theory," Joe said to Frank as they returned to their tents.

"Hi, guys," Michele Ebersol greeted them with a smile as they entered Ebersol's tent. Her pleasant expression quickly changed to one of surprise when she saw the man walking in behind them. "Tim!" she said. "What are you doing here?"

"I'm working on a documentary about the eclipse," he replied, returning her intent gaze. "But I'm only here because I was walking Joe and Frank back." He and Michele stared at each other, and Frank wished he knew what they were thinking.

"Well, um," Michele said after a pause, her voice a shade huskier than usual, "we'd better get back to work."

"Of course. Me, too." Abruptly, Tim turned and practically ran from the tent.

Michele watched him go before turning to the Hardys. "Where were you?" she asked. "I was about to send out a posse."

"It's a long story," Frank told her. "We'll tell you some other time."

"Hmmm. Sounds intriguing. But I wouldn't tell my husband you were with Tim Wheeler if I were you," she said, smiling sheepishly. "They're not the best of friends. Anyway, Jim

31

is off consulting with the observatory's meteorologist right now, and I think Everett is with a German research team. They should both be back any minute. I'd like to use this time to go over the setup with you. It's important that you know exactly what the sequence of events will be later today."

Michele stepped over to a long table at the front of the tent. It was covered with electronic equipment. In front of it was a director's chair with the words *Cosmic Explainer* stenciled on it.

"These machines will function as our main computer terminal," she explained as Frank and Joe listened intently. "All the data our infrared equipment generates in the aluminized tent will be fed in here through cables. Jim will stay here during the entire eclipse. He will read the data from Everett's detectors by watching this monitor. This other screen will show him what's coming in on the infrared video. The third screen will show the data digitally, and that machine will feed Jim a simultaneous printout. Got all that?"

Frank and Joe both nodded. "It sounds simple enough," Frank said.

"Good," she said, smiling. "Now let's go into the other tent."

"You mean the light-tight tent, right?" Frank asked.

"Right," Michele said, stepping from Ebersol's tent to the other one, about ten yards away. The Hardys followed her into the light lock, a small space with heavy black fabric flaps on either end. She closed the outer flap behind them, and suddenly the three of them were in pitch darkness.

"Whoa!" Frank exclaimed, surprised.

"This is to keep any light from seeping into the tent," Michele explained. "A single ray could destroy our film." She lifted the second flap, and they followed her into the tent.

"Brrrr!" Joe said, hugging himself as he stepped inside. "It's freezing in here."

Michele switched on a small desk lamp. "It has to be kept at a steady forty degrees Fahrenheit in here. The film is extremely heat-sensitive, so anything warmer could cloud the image it picks up."

"Remind me to bring my sweater," Joe told Frank.

"And don't forget, it will be pitch-dark while you're working," Michele went on. "You and Everett will be stationed here with your instruments. Feel free to watch the first stages of the eclipse from outside—wearing protective lenses, of course, so your eyes don't get damaged. But once we approach totality, stay inside until the eclipse is finished. That's vital. If any of us aren't positioned where we're supposed to be, we could blow the whole operation. You'll be able to communicate with me via this intercom, by the way. I'll have a walkie-talkie, so I'll hear you."

"Where will you be?" Frank asked her.

"I'll be outside between the tents, maintaining communications and taking photos. What you'll be seeing through your infrared lenses and what Dr. Ebersol sees on his monitors bear very little relation to what the eclipse looks like to the naked eye. We need to have some conventional photos, too." She stepped back from the brothers and gave them a dazzling smile before taking them back outside. "It's going to be fun, isn't it?"

Frank could see that Michele was tremendously excited about the eclipse, and her enthusiasm fired his own. "I can't wait," he told Joe as they stepped out of the tent into the sunshine.

Dr. Ebersol and Everett MacLaughlin were approaching from opposite directions. Ebersol came from the observatory, and MacLaughlin from the far side of the parking lot. Many of the foreign teams were positioned at that end.

"The weather conditions are perfect—not a cloud in the sky and none predicted," the famous scientist announced buoyantly, getting to them first.

"Great!" Michele replied. "The equipment is set up, and I've briefed the boys. All we have to do now is run our final checks."

"Hello, everyone," Everett said, joining the group. "Greetings from Dr. Weinschatz. I just was talking to him and his team. They're going to be measuring any changes in the earth's gravitational pull during the eclipse."

"Interesting," Ebersol said with a sly smile. "But not nearly so interesting as what we're up to. Right, boys?"

Frank and Joe smiled in reply. "How long do we have until the eclipse starts?" Frank asked.

MacLaughlin checked his watch. "One hour and forty-seven minutes, thirty-five seconds," he said.

"Give or take a nanosecond," Joe joked. Ebersol and Michele laughed, but Everett didn't seem to get the joke.

"He's kidding," Frank told the puzzled assistant.

"Oh!" MacLaughlin said, finally understanding. He chuckled weakly for their sake.

"Later today we'll know if you've been right about the missing planet, Jim," Michele said.

"It should be the biggest night of our lives," Ebersol agreed. Putting his arms around the shoulders of his wife and his assistant, he added, "If we're right about this, we'll go down in the history books."

"Well," Michele said with a wry smile. "*You* will anyway." Before he could react, she gave him a quick hug. "Which is fine with me, darling. I have all the fame I need just being married to you."

Frank noticed that her laughter and Everett's little chuckle after her joke were slightly forced. The Great Explainer wasn't uncomfortable at all, at least not visibly.

"Isn't she a darling?" Ebersol said proudly. "Between my lovely wife and my loyal assistant, I have to say I am one very lucky astrophysicist. But enough sentiment," he added quickly. "Let's get to work!"

The eclipse began at 5:17 P.M. Donning goggles with dark protective lenses designed especially for looking at the sun, the Hardys gazed at the fantastic event in the heavens above them. The blazing disc of the sun began to fall into shadow as the moon's orbit placed it directly between the sun and the earth. Minute by minute, the sun grew smaller until, about forty minutes after the eclipse had begun, it resembled a fiery crescent moon.

"It won't be long now," Michele said as their little group stared up at the sky together.

"It's just unreal!" Joe enthused. "Can you believe this, Frank?"

"I feel incredibly lucky to be here," Frank said, but was haunted by the sudden remembrance of what Dr. Ebersol had said about an eclipse being an evil omen. The careening van hurtled again through the back of his mind. So did the image of Ebersol's hand frozen to the mike short-circuiting. Frank hoped those events were nothing sinister.

All over the mountaintop groups of people were headed into the main observatory, the many smaller buildings, and their makeshift trailers and tents. "Most of these people are here to study the sun's corona and its flares," Ebersol explained, following Frank's glance. "Our work doesn't begin until the eclipse becomes total."

Raising his eyes to the sun again, Frank saw that the last sliver of the sun was about to disappear behind the moon. Small beads of fire encircled the black disc at the center. "Bailey's Beads," Michele said aloud. "Beautiful, aren't they? Like a crown of fire."

In an instant the fiery beads were gone, too, and although it was only five-thirty on a midsummer day, the stars were suddenly fully visible. "This is it!" Michele cried out. "Everyone to battle stations!"

Ebersol's little group hurried into their

tents—all except Michele, who remained outside.

Inside the aluminized tent it was pitch-dark and noisy from the hum of the air conditioners. Frank had to feel his way to his chair, which had been strategically placed in front of the infrared camera on its mount. He pulled off his solar goggles and peered into the lens, aiming it at the eclipsed sun. He pressed the shutter, and the camera's motor drive whirred into action, snapping picture after picture.

"Are you okay, Everett?" Joe asked. Joe had arrived at his position directly behind Frank, a second camera with extra film ready for quick reloading in the dark.

The graduate assistant's reply was a terse "Please don't talk to me during operations. I need my full concentration." Frank heard him stumble over to his seat, where, through rubber-framed goggles, he could observe the data from his infrared detectors on a computer screen.

As soon as Frank finished a roll of film, he unsnapped the camera from its base and handed it to Joe. Joe then handed him the second loaded camera. Frank snapped it onto the base and set the motor drive in motion.

Over the intercom, Michele's voice crackled, informing them about the eclipse's progress.

"I never realized how long seven minutes could be," Joe said.

When Bailey's Beads returned, Michele informed them that the eclipse was over. Frank and Joe stopped shooting. In the dark they stowed their film in a light-tight, refrigerated thermos bag.

"Whew," Frank said, putting the canister into a cooler on the floor. Behind them, he heard MacLaughlin shuffling around at his station. "That was great, Joe, but I'm glad it's over. I was afraid something might go wrong, and it'd be our fault."

"Well, relax," Joe said as they moved out into the light lock, giving each other tired high fives. "Nothing can go wrong now."

Just as he said the words a scream rose from outside, from the direction of the main tent.

"He's dead!" Michele Ebersol's anguished voice cried out. "You killed him!"

Chapter

4

STUMBLING OUT of the light lock into the open air, the Hardys heard Michele scream again. Joe saw her standing in the doorway of the other tent, her hand covering her mouth.

Joe and Frank rushed to her in the growing light. Frank pulled her away from the tent opening as Joe peered inside. There he saw Tim Wheeler kneeling over the prone, blood-soaked body of Dr. Ebersol! A bloody knife was in Wheeler's hand.

Joe didn't wait. Lunging at Wheeler, he hit him in the jaw with a sharp right that flattened the reporter. By the time Joe had made sure Wheeler was unconscious, Frank was kneeling over Ebersol, feeling for a pulse. He shook his head sadly.

As Michele leaned on a tent pole for support, Everett MacLaughlin poked his head in through the tent opening. "Is something the matter?" he asked.

"Call an ambulance!" Joe cried. "Get the police, too! Dr. Ebersol's been stabbed!"

"What?" the stunned assistant gasped, staring at the body of his mentor on the floor. Then he backed out of the tent, saying, "I'll get help."

Joe stared at Ebersol's lifeless form. It was hard to believe, hard to take it all in. Joe and his brother had been only yards away from a brutal murder. Yet they'd been so absorbed in the celestial event taking place millions of miles away that the slaying had occurred without their knowing it.

"This should have been his moment of triumph," Michele sobbed.

Minutes later police and ambulance helicopters arrived, and the tent was soon filled with police and paramedics, who confirmed the obvious—Ebersol was dead. Hearing this, Michele burst into a fresh round of sobbing, while MacLaughlin stood staring at the body, obviously in shock.

The police captain, a handsome man of about thirty, with a square, flat face, long black hair, powerful frame, and penetrating gaze, asked Michele what had happened. "When I came in here I found my husband dead," she answered tear-

41

fully. "Mr. Wheeler was right beside him, holding a knife."

"Cuff him," the captain told his assistants.

Wheeler's eyes fluttered open just as cuffs snapped shut around his wrists.

"You are under arrest for the murder of Dr. James Ebersol," the captain told him. "You have the right to remain silent, the right to counsel, and anything you say can and will be held against you. Understand?"

"What?" Wheeler asked frantically, staring at the police captain. "But I didn't kill him! I came in to interview him, and I found him like that. I picked up the knife, and the next thing I knew, someone socked me. That's the last I remember!" Wheeler's panic-stricken eyes darted from Michele to the Hardys to MacLaughlin and to the police. "You've got to believe me—I didn't kill him!"

The police captain was not buying Wheeler's story. "Looks pretty open and shut to me," he said. Turning to Joe, he asked, "What's your name, and what are you doing here?"

"I'm Joe Hardy," he replied. "My brother Frank and I were assisting Dr. Ebersol during the eclipse. We were in the next tent with Mr. MacLaughlin."

"Did either of you see anyone go into or out of this tent during the eclipse?" the captain asked.

"No, sir," Joe told him,

"I see," the captain replied crisply, making a note. "And do you happen to know of any dispute or hard feelings between Mr. Wheeler and Dr. Ebersol?"

"Well," Joe began reluctantly, "Mr. Wheeler was pretty open about not liking Dr. Ebersol."

"But I wouldn't rush to any conclusions, officer," Frank interrupted quickly. "Mr. Wheeler doesn't seem like the kind of man who'd—"

"I'll ask the questions, if you don't mind," the captain said, cutting him off.

"Of course," Frank said, backing down and feeling like a total idiot.

"Officer, my brother Frank and I are here as Dr. Ebersol's assistants, but we're detectives back home," Joe offered. "If we can help . . ."

"We'll see," the captain told him. "My name's Kanekahana, by the way." Then he turned to Everett MacLaughlin and asked, "Who are you, and how did you get here?"

"I'm Everett MacLaughlin, Dr. Ebersol's assistant," MacLaughlin answered. Frank noticed that his eyes were still fixed on Ebersol's dead body, which was now being put into a body bag by the paramedics.

"Were you aware of any problem between the doctor and this man here?" the captain asked, indicating Wheeler with a toss of his head.

"The only thing I know is that Mr. Wheeler

was once engaged to Mrs. Ebersol," MacLaughlin said.

"Is that so?" the captain asked, nodding his head. "Very interesting."

"Captain, we need to give Mrs. Ebersol a sedative," one of the paramedics said, her arm around the dead scientist's sobbing wife.

The captain waved his hand. "Fine, fine. I have all I want right now anyway. Get Wheeler out of here, too. We'll take him with us when we go back to headquarters."

Outside, Frank could hear reporters calling out questions to the police and paramedics. He guessed that most of them had been at the observatory to write about the solar eclipse. Now they had a very different story to report.

"Okay, everyone—please step outside, but don't go too far. We need to dust this area for prints," one of the officers directed.

Frank noticed that Everett MacLaughlin wasn't responding to the woman's command. "Come on, Mr. MacLaughlin," he said, giving him a light tap on the shoulder. "We have to go now."

"He's dead. . . ." MacLaughlin whispered, still staring at the spot where the body had lain. "He's actually dead."

"Come on, pal," Joe urged, gently pushing him out of the tent.

"Here's the plan, people," the captain announced to the assembled group once they were all out of the tent. "I'm setting up shop in the administration office, that white building across the parking lot. First, I'll deal with Mr. Wheeler and confer with my staff. Next I'll speak with Mr. MacLaughlin. That should be in about twenty minutes. Joe and Frank Hardy, come by after that in, say, forty minutes."

Frank and Joe watched as Ebersol's body was loaded aboard a helicopter for transit back to the morgue in Kailua, and the police cordoned off the tent with yellow tape. The eclipse was almost completely over now, and the sun, almost back to its full size, was reaching toward the horizon.

"Hey, you two!" a voice called out to them. "Weren't you Ebersol's assistants?" Joe saw that the voice belonged to a reporter, one of a small group who were moving toward them. "What happened in there?"

"Sorry," Frank told them. "We'll do our talking to the police."

"Suit yourself," said the reporter. "Come on, gang," he said. "Let's go see if we can talk to Tim Wheeler before they haul him off to jail." With that, they took off for the white building.

"Well," Joe said to Frank, "it looks like a pretty open-and-shut case, huh?"

"I guess so," Frank said, scuffing up the dirt beneath his feet.

"It only could have been him," Joe pointed out. "Everyone else was totally occupied during the eclipse. Wheeler was the only one around our tents without a specific job during those seven minutes."

"I suppose so," Frank said, sounding unconvinced.

"Not to mention the fact that Michele found him with the knife in his hand, leaning over the body. Say, Frank, do you think he exposed that wire the other night, too?"

"I don't know," Frank said slowly. "But something about all this doesn't feel right. How could it have been Wheeler in the van earlier today? He was right behind us on his bicycle."

"The van could have just had bad brakes," Joe suggested.

"You didn't think so at the time," Frank reminded him. "Besides, you heard Wheeler. He's claiming he wandered in there and found the body. It's possible he's telling the truth, isn't it?"

"Oh, come on, Frank!" Joe protested as they walked across the parking lot to the white building. "You heard him say he hated Ebersol. He had a motive, he had opportunity, and if that knife wasn't the means, my name's not Joe Hardy!"

"True," Frank reluctantly agreed. "Still, I

have a hunch Wheeler's not the type to go around stabbing people."

Two police officers were emerging from the white building now, leading Tim Wheeler in handcuffs toward a helicopter that was just in front of Frank and Joe. Reporters swarmed around, taking pictures and shouting questions in vain. Moments later the chopper took off, sending a cloud of dust shooting out toward the Hardys. Frank and Joe had to turn away, and ended up squinting into the setting sun.

"Hey!" Frank shouted, pointing toward the aluminized tent. "Look over there!"

"What the—?" Joe asked, following his brother's gaze. Someone was coming out of their tent, carrying a small bag. With the sun in their eyes, Joe and Frank found it impossible to identify who it was. The silhouetted figure was making for one of the trails that led down the mountain. "Let's go check this out," Joe said, rushing toward the tent.

Joe had thrown the flaps aside and entered the tent just as Frank came up behind him.

"Joe!" Frank said, sweeping the interior with his gaze. "The refrigerated bag with our film is gone!"

"Come on," Joe cried, sprinting out of the tent again. "Maybe we can catch up with whoever took it!"

Outside, Frank bumped into a worried-looking paramedic. "Michele Ebersol is missing," she told Frank. "Have you seen her?"

"Sorry, we haven't," Frank told the woman. Turning to Joe, he added, "Maybe she took our film, Joe. Come on!"

"I'm with you," Joe said, bolting for the trail.

The footpath was narrow and steep, and the brothers had to move single file, with Joe a few steps in the lead. They were expert climbers, though, and soon heard someone moving around the bend just in front of them.

Joe rounded the corner carefully. At this point on the trail, the cliff dropped off on his left for about thirty feet straight down, while thick branches intruded on the right. He maneuvered his way through them, thinking how odd it was that the footsteps ahead of him had stopped.

Then, suddenly, he knew why. A leg shot out from the undergrowth, sending him sprawling headlong toward the edge of the path.

"Frank! Heeellp!" Joe shouted too late. He was already going over the edge!

Chapter

5

FRANK ROUNDED the bend in time to see Joe's feet disappearing over the edge of the embankment. He dove, grasping for them, but came up with nothing. Joe's scream died in the air as Frank winced, shutting his eyes.

"Joe!" he shouted, scrambling to peer over the edge. "Joe, are you okay?"

Thirty feet below him, Frank saw his brother, entangled in the underbrush. Joe wasn't moving.

"Joe!" Frank yelled again. The slope was steep, but using handholds in the jutting rock, Frank was able to make his own way down. By the time he got there, Joe was stirring. He was alive, at least. Frank lifted Joe out of his

49

tangle and laid him down on his back in the grass.

"Oooohh," Joe groaned. "Everything hurts. Frank, is that you?"

"It's me, Joe," Frank said, kneeling beside him. "Do you think you broke anything?" Joe had a deep gash on his forearm and a big bruise on his cheek.

"I don't think so. You know I didn't just fall, someone tried to kill me! They put out a leg and tripped me," Joe said, wincing. "I slowed my fall by grabbing that branch up there." He pointed up to where a brush grew straight out of the side of the embankment. Then he raised himself to his elbows. "Rats!" he muttered, "I can't stand the idea that someone got away with our film! Do you realize this could be the end of the exploded planet theory? It makes me sick even to think about it!"

"I know how you feel, but there's not much we can do about it now. Come on, let me help you. We've got to get you back up to the observatory."

"Is my face totally swollen?" Joe asked, worried.

"You got a bad bruise," Frank told him. "That gash on your arm is pretty nasty, too. Let's get you back topside."

It took a while for them to scramble back

up the embankment, with Joe groaning all the way that his whole body ached. "We'll get you a hot bath back at the hotel," Frank told him.

"We're supposed to call Mom and Dad tomorrow morning and tell them how things went," Joe said anxiously. "They're not going to like it that we've gotten into so much trouble."

"The news of Ebersol's murder is going to be on TV and in all the papers," Frank replied. "There's no way to keep them in the dark. But if it makes you happy, we won't say anything about this little accident."

"Accident! I told you, somebody tripped me," Joe cried, stopping on the footpath as they neared the observatory compound.

"I heard you, and I do believe you," Frank said. "So I guess whoever stole our film is even willing to kill to keep it—which makes me wonder about Tim Wheeler. He couldn't have tripped you—he's in police custody."

"That's true!" Joe said, realizing that Frank was right. "Come on, let's go tell that police captain. He's waiting to interview us anyway."

Captain Kanekahana was not impressed with the Hardys' story. "Look, guys," he told them. "I'll tell you now what I didn't mention when I first met you: I've heard of you and your father. You've got great reputations, and I've got all the respect in the world for you. But I've got to be frank—I don't see any possible connection between the Ebersol murder and what just happened on the path. I've got a pretty good murder suspect already in custody."

"How can you say that?" Joe asked as a paramedic applied a butterfly bandage to the gash on his forearm. "We told you about the van attempting to run us down. That couldn't have been Wheeler either!"

"True," the captain admitted. "But it could have been a case of bad brakes. As for the theft of your film, I can think of lots of reasons for someone to steal it."

"Such as?" Frank asked.

"Such as the fact that this mountaintop is full of scientists who would love to present that film as the product of their own research. And there are a fair number of media people up here, too. One of them could have taken it to back up a scoop about the discovery of the missing planet or to add an original angle on Ebersol's murder. Hey, someone could even have snatched the film as a souvenir."

"We should have thought of those possibilities," Frank admitted.

"Hold on a minute, Captain," Joe said, sounding annoyed. "Whoever stole that film wanted to keep it badly enough to risk killing me. That doesn't sound like a souvenir hunter to me—or a reporter trying to get a scoop."

Kanekahana frowned. "It's entirely possible that the 'leg' you tripped over was really a branch or vine, Joe."

"No way," Joe insisted. "Whatever tripped me was thick, Captain. As thick as a human leg."

"One of the paramedics told us that Michele was missing," Frank said, trying to get some useful information. "Have you found her yet?"

"She just wandered away for a few minutes," the captain said. "After she refused a sedative, she said she wanted to be by herself—which is totally understandable to me. The woman just lost her husband."

"But she was missing at the same time that someone tripped me," Joe reasoned.

"Please, I have enough trouble right now without searching for more," the captain said with an impatient sigh. "Right now I've got a murder case on my hands. My plan is to get a confession from Wheeler by tonight, and once that's wrapped up, I'll help you find your film."

Joe started to protest, but Frank put a hand on his shoulder. "Forget it, Joe," he said. "It's no use. The captain's mind is made up, and nothing we can say is going to change it."

"That's right," Kanekahana said, nodding and smiling. "And I advise you boys to stay out of trouble. Come by the station in the morning and sign your statements about the theft. I promise we'll be on it the minute I get Wheeler squared away. Take it easy, okay? Everything is in capable hands, so you two can relax and enjoy your vacation in Hawaii."

Outside again, Joe turned to Frank and asked, "What do we do now?"

Instead of answering, Frank motioned for Joe to follow him. He led his brother back inside the aluminized tent. There he felt inside the camera and pulled out the roll of film. "Just as I thought!" he said excitedly. "The thief missed our last roll of film—the one that was left in the camera!"

"All right!" Joe said. "Maybe our luck is turning."

"We'd better hope it turns," Frank said, "before it runs out altogether."

By the time Frank and Joe got back to their hotel, it was past nine o'clock, and the stars were out. The hotel pool was still open, and since it had a whirlpool attached to it, Frank and Joe decided that a swim and a soak would be better for Joe's aches and pains than a hot bath. Putting the roll of film in the small refrigerator in their second-floor room, they changed into bathing suits and went downstairs.

As they sat in the whirlpool, Joe said, "I

don't think a lot of that police captain. He seems awfully arrogant to me."

"I know," Frank agreed, tapping his fingers on his leg. "And awfully anxious for a quick arrest, too. I'd hate to be Tim Wheeler tonight."

"But, Frank," Joe said, "if the murderer isn't Wheeler, who is it?"

Frank thought hard. "I don't know. But I'll tell you one thing. I thought it was interesting that Michele Ebersol was missing at the same time our film was stolen. And when you think about it, she was alone out there during the eclipse, right outside Ebersol's tent. Why didn't she see anyone go in or out?"

"Are you saying she killed her own husband?" Joe asked, incredulous.

"It's been known to happen, Joe," Frank commented. "Hey, are you as hungry as I am? We forgot all about dinner."

"Famished," Joe said, lifting himself out of the whirlpool. "Boy, I feel a lot better. Let's go get some grub!"

The brothers went back to their room to change, then headed out onto the main commercial boulevard. There they found a crowded fish restaurant, The Tradewinds, and squeezed into a corner table.

After a dinner of *mahi mahi*, a local fish delicacy, and *poi*, a native Hawaiian staple, the brothers headed back to their hotel room for a good night's sleep.

"I'm ready to collapse," Frank confessed.

"Me, too," Joe agreed. "It's been quite a day." He fished out the key and unlocked the door to their room. "Hey, Frank, do you think—"

Joe froze in the doorway, Frank right behind him, staring into the darkness of their room. Inside, he could just make out what had made Joe stop short.

It was the figure of a man!

"There's a killer on the loose," said a voice in the darkness. "Take my word for it, you're the next victims."

Chapter

6

BOTH BOYS BRACED for an attack. Joe clenched his fists, and Frank went into a deep karate horse stance. Reaching over, Joe quickly flicked on the light.

"Wheeler!" he gasped. The reporter stood facing them, his face white. He held his hands up in front of him. At least he's unarmed, Joe thought.

"What are you doing here?" Frank wanted to know. He relaxed his aggressive stance, but only slightly. "How did you get out of police custody?"

"I came here to tell you the truth," Wheeler said. "I didn't kill Ebersol. You've got to believe me. Please, I need your help!"

"If you didn't, who did?" Joe broke in.

"How should I know?" Wheeler insisted. "But I'll tell you what I do know—whoever did it is desperate enough to kill anyone who gets in the way, including you."

"You still haven't answered my questions," Frank pointed out.

"My film company bailed me out," Wheeler explained. "But not before that police captain grilled me for two hours. He wasn't even going to take me before a judge for a bail hearing, except that I had no criminal record, there was no physical evidence to connect me to the murder—"

"What about the knife in your hand?" Joe challenged him. "That seems pretty physical to me."

"I told you, I picked it up off the floor. It was a stupid thing to do. But there was no blood on the rest of me. If I'd killed him, I'd have been covered with it. Even the police captain could see that. He didn't want to let me go, I could tell. For all I know he's probably got someone following me."

"Why did you come here, then?" Frank asked.

"Yeah," Joe echoed. "You say you have no criminal record, but I'd say this looks like breaking and entering."

"Come on, Joe. I *had* to talk to you,"

Wheeler said. "You two are detectives. You've got to figure out who really killed Ebersol!"

"Suppose we do help you," Frank said, sitting on the arm of the sofa. "If we agree, you've got to start by telling us everything you know."

"About what?" Wheeler asked.

"About Ebersol, and his wife, and staff, anything that might shed light on why he was murdered," Frank explained.

Wheeler let out a deep sigh. "For starters, you might be interested to know that I saw Ebersol last night."

"What?" Joe asked. "But when he left us, he and his wife were headed for their beach house to meet with some benefactors. It was already pretty late, too. Were you there?"

"No," Wheeler replied. "I met him at the lounge in my hotel—the Paradiso, a few blocks up Kailua strip. It was about eleven-thirty, I think."

"Did you talk to him?" Frank asked.

"Did I ever!" Wheeler gave a mirthless little laugh. "I poked so many holes in his exploded planet theory it ended up like a sieve. And the funny thing is, once I got going, he didn't argue with me. It was as if he didn't know his own work! Either that or his mind was a million miles away."

"Why would a man leave his beautiful wife

to hang out in a hotel lounge at eleven o'clock at night?" Frank wondered out loud.

"Maybe they had a fight?" Wheeler suggested.

"Tell us about Michele, Tim," Joe said. "What's she really like?"

"That's tough," Wheeler said, frowning. "She's the type of person who will be sweet as pie one minute and stab you in the back the next."

"Did you say 'stab in the back'?" Frank said, raising an eyebrow.

"I didn't mean it literally," Wheeler protested. "The thought of Michele murdering anyone is absurd. Which isn't to say she doesn't have her downside. She can be extremely ambitious, ruthless even—especially when it comes to money. That girl loves money and the things it can buy. Of course, she's pretty fond of power and prestige, too."

Wheeler shook his head sadly, a pained expression on his face.

"Do you think she killed him?" Frank asked bluntly.

"I can't bring myself to believe it," the writer said with a shiver. "But I suppose she could have. Think about the way it's all going to wind up—Michele will take over Ebersol's research, probably get to run the foundation, and inherit all his book royalties while I'm doing prison time!"

Frank and Joe looked at each other dubiously. Could Wheeler be telling the truth? Joe wondered. Or was he just making it up about Michele to throw suspicion on someone other than himself?

"All right, Wheeler," Frank said. "We'll look into all this. In the meantime I suggest you stay right where the police can see you. When we find something out, we'll come to you."

"Thank you," the frightened reporter said, getting up to go. "I can't thank you guys enough."

"You're right about that," Frank said grimly. "You can't."

The next morning before breakfast Frank and Joe tapped on Everett MacLaughlin's door. But the assistant wasn't there.

"He's probably at the observatory already, going over the data we got during the eclipse," Frank said.

"Yeah," Joe agreed. "I don't think Mac-Laughlin would let a little thing like a murder stop him from the pursuit of science."

The brothers had fresh papaya and watermelon salad with macadamia nut muffins for breakfast. Then they went back to their room to call home. Their father had been called away on a case unexpectedly, but Laura Hardy was waiting for their call.

"I was worried when I heard about what happened to Dr. Ebersol," Laura Hardy said. "But I understand they caught the killer—some love-crazed reporter."

"Mom, have you been reading the papers?" Joe asked, surprised.

"No, it was on TV, Joe," she replied.

"Well, don't believe everything you see on TV," Joe told her.

"You know I don't," she replied, sounding a little embarrassed. "Listen, I want you boys to take care of yourselves, okay? Just because there's trouble doesn't mean you have to get involved."

"We'll be careful, Mom," Joe said in a friendly, teasing tone. "Promise."

"Oh, there's no sense talking to you or your father about things like that," she admitted. "Just come home in one piece. Okay?"

Their next stop was the police station, where they filed a formal complaint about the stolen film.

"I hated to let Wheeler go free," Captain Kanekahana complained.

" 'Innocent until proven guilty,' right, Captain?" Frank reminded him gently.

The captain nodded reluctantly and turned

his attention back to the form they'd filed. The brothers had decided earlier not to mention the roll of film they'd salvaged from the camera, which was now safe in the refrigerator of their room. They didn't tell him about their meeting with Wheeler, either. If Kanekahana knew about either of those things, he'd probably confiscate their film, order them off the case, and put a police surveillance team on them. That would be the end of their own investigation.

"It's kind of hard to estimate the value of the film," Joe told the captain, "so we left that blank."

"No problem," Kanekahana told them. "That question is more for the insurance people than for the police. But remember, I warned you. The film theft is low priority around here. I can't really get to it until the murder is wrapped up."

"That's okay, Captain," Joe said politely. "We appreciate whatever help you can give us."

"Okay," the captain said, rising and walking them to the door. "I want you guys to stay out of trouble now."

"We want to stay out of trouble," Frank replied, grinning. "Have a good day, Captain."

The moment they left the building, however,

thcy went searching for the very kind of trouble they'd been warned against.

"Okay, Michele, we're on our way," Joe joked as their red convertible sped along the sparkling, sunlit coast toward the Ebersols' rented beach house.

The house was set back from the road and down a steep hill fringed by tropical vegetation—mostly palms and cactus here on the dry side of Big Island. "Wow, this place is something else," Frank said, letting out a low whistle as he parked along the road.

"It doesn't get better than this," Joe agreed, taking in the long, low white stucco structure set on a lonely stretch of perfect white sand.

"This sure beats our budget hotel," Joe commented. He couldn't help comparing their accommodations and these. Had Ebersol made arrangements or had Michele? Joe wondered, thinking of what Wheeler had told them.

They rang the bell, but there was no answer. "That's funny," Frank said. He and Joe had seen the Ebersols' luxury convertible with rental plates parked in the driveway.

"Maybe she's out on the beach in back," Joe suggested. The brothers went around the side of the house. As they passed the pool, Joe noticed a large towel draped over a chair. But no Michele. "Maybe she went for a walk," Joe added.

"I guess we'll have to come back later," Frank said, scanning the empty beach.

They were just leaving when Joe spotted something out in the ocean—about a hundred yards out, by his best guess.

"I see a surfboard," he said to Frank, who was also focusing on it now. "Someone's lying on it." Joe had his hand at his forehead, shielding his eyes from the sun. The figure on the surfboard was motionless, in a facedown position. Joe turned to his brother, his eyes widening. "That's got to be Michele," he said.

Frank nodded grimly. "And the tide is taking her right out to sea!"

Chapter

7

"MRS. EBERSOL!" Frank called out, cupping his hands to his mouth. Joe joined him. The two of them called her name several times as loudly as they could. The figure on the surfboard didn't move. She was drifting farther out to sea with every passing moment.

"Let's go after her," Joe said, starting to strip down to his shorts. Frank ran to the poolhouse and came out with a surfboard under each arm. Soon the boys were wading into the ocean and paddling seaward.

After a few minutes they were close enough to see Michele's red hair and the fact that she was unconscious. She seemed to be floating in a faster current than they were in, because the

Hardys had to paddle as hard as they could to continue to gain ground.

After what seemed an hour, they caught up to Michele Ebersol. "I thought we were going to lose her," Frank confessed, as Joe felt for a pulse.

"She's alive," he told Frank. Each brother grabbed her surfboard with one hand and, paddling with the other, headed back toward shore. It was even harder to make progress since the current was against them.

"Let's head to that beach over there," Joe called out, indicating a strip of sand to their right, more or less in the direction they were being pulled. As they paddled along, using the current to their advantage, Michele Ebersol began to stir.

"Ohhh . . ." she moaned groggily. "Ohhh . . ."

"She sounds like she's been drugged," Frank observed. "I'll bet somebody gave her something to knock her out, just long enough for the tide to take her out to sea. If we hadn't come along when we did . . ." Frank swallowed hard, thinking about the terrible possibility of two deaths in two days.

As they neared the beach, Frank and Joe got off their boards and waded in the rest of the way. Then they started walking Michele back toward her house, leaving the boards where they'd come ashore.

"Do you think she needs a doctor?" Joe

asked. The scientist was stumbling badly, even though she had one arm on each of their shoulders.

"Let's see how she is once we get her inside," Frank said.

Fortunately, the french doors that connected the veranda to the house were unlocked. They led Michele inside, walked her to one of the long white leather couches in the sunken living room, and helped her to lie down. Frank spotted a couple of beach towels on the dining table and wrapped them around her.

"Mrs. Ebersol? Can you hear me?" Joe asked, standing over her.

The only reply he got was a slight nod of her head. Her eyes remained shut and her limbs appeared to be as weak as a rag doll's.

"Maybe some coffee will help," Frank suggested. He glanced at the countertop island between the dining area and kitchen. "There's some in a pot over there."

At that, Michele raised her head and shook it slightly. "No," she groaned, her beautiful brown eyes fluttering open slowly. "No coffee."

Frank and Joe were encouraged. Michele was going to be okay.

"Richard . . ." she mumbled under her breath. "Why, Richard?"

"Who's Richard, Mrs. Ebersol?" Joe asked,

hoping for a lead while her defenses were down.

"Richard De La Rosa," Michele said, not really noticing Joe. "He should be in jail." She shut her eyes and lay back down, taking a deep breath.

"I've heard that name before," Joe said. "He works for the foundation, right, Mrs. Ebersol?"

"Calls himself our manager," she replied, struggling to sit up. "Couldn't manage a baseball team, let alone a scientific foundation," she murmured. "Don't know why Jim didn't fire him months ago." Now she leaned forward, her elbows on her knees, and gave a little shiver. "He should go to jail—"

"Why should he go to jail?" Joe asked gently.

"You ask him—just ask him. Richard De La Rosa is a thief. He's always wasting the foundation's money. Flew in from L.A. last night. That's another airfare we have to pay. He probably steals from the foundation, too. I warned Jim about it. There's been a lot of money missing—"

"Is that why he should go to jail?" Frank asked. "Because he stole the foundation's money?"

"You ask him," she replied, staring at Frank with unfocused eyes. "He's staying at your hotel."

"This missing money," Joe said. "Can you tell us anything more about it?"

"That's what he and I were talking about this morning before— How did I get in the water? I didn't go for a swim." The look on her face was one of sheer confusion. It was obvious to Joe that she hadn't a clue about what had happened to her.

"Tell us more about the money," Frank said gently. "Maybe we can help you if we know more."

"The money was for scientific research," she told them. "But what's the difference? It's gone now. The money's gone—"

"All of it?" Frank asked.

"Most," she said, appearing more alert all at once. "Well, I'll fix that. As soon as I take over officially, Richard De La Rosa will be out. Everett MacLaughlin, too—that idiot. He came by at breakfast time. All he wanted to talk about was the eclipse. As if Jim hadn't died yesterday. As if I needed the little twerp to move on with the next step—"

"What next step?" Joe wanted to know.

"The book, of course!" she replied, surprised that he had even asked. "A best-selling book on the exploded planet theory. Jim started it months ago."

"But we don't know yet whether there was a planet or not," Joe said. "Everett MacLaughlin is probably trying to sort that out right now."

"I hate to give you more bad news, Mrs. Ebersol, but someone stole our infrared film," Joe told her, searching her face to see what her response might be. To his surprise, she didn't seem upset in the least.

"It doesn't matter," she insisted. "It'll be a best-seller anyhow. The theory's so interesting, don't you think? Besides, it's Jim's last book— it'll sell a million copies at least. And MacLaughlin's name is not going to be on it. I'm not even going to credit him. He's been such a nuisance the whole time. Jim isn't here to protect him anymore. Poor Jim . . ." Her eyes welled up with tears, and she shut them again.

"Mrs. Ebersol," Joe said, "are you absolutely sure you didn't take anything today? Medication of any kind?"

"The paramedics wanted to give me something yesterday, but I refused and walked away from them," she said, stopping for a moment. "When they found me, they gave me a bottle to take home. Last night I might have taken a sedative—frankly, I forget." After going into the bathroom, she came back out with a bottle of pills. "They gave me twenty and there are only eighteen in here," she said. "I guess I did take a couple, though I don't have any memory of it."

"Did you drink anything when Mr. De La Rosa was here?" Frank asked.

"Oh, yes," she said. "We had iced tea. Richard mixed it up for us." Frank and Joe's eyes met, and each raised an eyebrow.

"It's late," Michele announced in a tone that indicated to Frank that she was fully recovered. "I have a lot to do. Would you mind leaving now."

"Are you sure you're all right?" Frank asked.

"Yes, I'm sure," she said, giving him a tense smile. "Don't worry. I won't take any more pills, that's for sure."

"Aren't you at least going to inform the police of what has happened?" Joe asked.

"And tell them what?" she asked, her brown eyes widening. "I don't know what happened." She walked to the front door and opened it. A definite cue for them to leave. "See you up at the observatory," she said. "Oh, and thanks for saving my life."

Frank and Joe were driving down the road, headed for Kailua, before either of them said a word.

"Wow," Joe finally remarked. "That was pretty strange behavior, wasn't it? Anger, grief, and greed all mixed together."

"I'll say," Frank agreed, his hands tight on the steering wheel. "What got me was that Michele seemed much more concerned about who controls Dr. Ebersol's work and the foundation money than she did with the fact that he's dead."

"Well, the situation seems pretty clear to me," Joe said. "Someone—maybe that guy De La Rosa—drugged Michele and shoved her out to sea to cover up his murder of Ebersol, and maybe the theft of the foundation's funds, too."

"Whoa!" Frank said, laughing. "Slow down, Joe. We don't know for sure that Michele was drugged. We certainly don't know by whom. She might have taken those two pills and had a bad reaction, maybe from stress. Besides, according to her, De La Rosa flew in last night. If that's true, he wasn't even around when Ebersol was murdered."

"We can check on that," Joe said. "But he drugged her for sure. Didn't you see how she was acting? One sedative wouldn't make a person behave like that. It would have taken at least a couple."

"It could have been an act, too. For all we know, Michele killed her husband and is now trying to put the blame on someone else—just in case they can't pin the murder on Wheeler, I guess," Frank said, reviewing the possibilities. "Remember—she may be the one who stole our film."

"I think we ought to tell the police what

happened today," Joe said. "Maybe they'll want to send someone to protect Michele? Seems to me she's making a lot of enemies—Wheeler, MacLaughlin, De La Rosa . . ."

"I'm not sure calling the police would do any good," Frank said. "Michele would only deny she was drugged, and Kanekahana has already told us to keep out of trouble. Anyhow, I think we have to talk to De La Rosa first."

Frank was lost in thought as he drove down the Kailua strip. "I'll tell you one thing, Joe—that woman is hiding something important. And we've got to find out what it is."

Back at their hotel, they parked the car and went to the lobby, where they got Richard De La Rosa's room number from the clerk at the front desk. His room was on the third floor in the back, overlooking the pool. "Now let's remember to be nice to this guy," Frank told his brother. "He could be the key to the whole case."

"I say we have to check out his time of arrival in Hawaii," Joe said.

"We will," Frank assured him. "Later."

When the Hardys got to the room, they were surprised to find that the door was slightly ajar. Peeking inside, Joe saw that the bed was made and that there were no luggage and personal items around. "The room's empty," he said to Frank.

"Maybe" was all Frank said. Both brothers knew that, after the events of the past twenty-four hours, they couldn't walk away without having a quick look inside. Frank gestured for Joe to go in first. Joe opened the door, slipping silently inside with Frank right behind him.

The room seemed empty. The brothers tiptoed around, glancing in all directions for any sign of habitation. Frank saw Joe turn the corner to the bathroom area and started to follow him.

Frank was caught up short when he heard Joe gasp. He stood stock-still for a long moment, listening, but there was no further sound. "Joe?" he called out. "Joe, are you all right?"

Before Frank knew what was happening, Joe came back around the corner. His eyes were opened wide, and there was a gun at his head! The man holding the pistol emerged from behind the partition, his face tense with anger and fear.

"I knew she'd send someone after me!" he growled. "I was ready for you! Ha! Now get out of here. Go tell Michele I didn't take the money!" he shouted to Frank, a crazed expression on his face. "Get out now, or I'll kill you both!"

Chapter

8

FRANK'S MIND was racing. The man certainly seemed capable of blowing Joe's brains out. "Er, Mr. De La Rosa?" Frank began.

"She sent you, didn't she?" the man asked. "Admit it, or I'll blow your friend to smithereens!"

"No, sir," Frank said, trying to keep his voice steady. "We came on our own."

"Don't give me that baloney!" De La Rosa said, momentarily waving the gun Frank's way before putting it back to Joe's temple. "She's out to get me, and that's why you're here. Now you're going to tell me everything you know!"

Frank nodded and said, "First of all, my brother and I were asked by Dr. Ebersol to be assistants at the eclipse. Then, when he was murdered, we decided to investigate. We have some experience as detectives, you see. So we went out to the Ebersols' house this morning to talk to Michele."

"Aha!" De La Rosa shouted. "I knew it! And then she sent you to search my room, right?"

"No, sir," Frank insisted, trying to stay calm. "If you'll just put that gun away, we can discuss this like human—"

"Shut up!" De La Rosa ordered. "No way I'm putting this gun down till I get some answers!"

"I'd just like to remind you, sir, that what you're doing is against the law. I'm sure you don't want to make trouble for yourself down the road." Frank watched De La Rosa to see what effect his words were having. If the man had already killed Ebersol, being charged with another crime wouldn't faze him. On the other hand, if he had only stolen money, he might not want to be charged with a violent crime as well.

"Talk," De La Rosa said, still holding the gun to Joe's head. "What did she say about me?"

"She said you belonged in jail!" Joe retorted. "She told us to ask you why. Care to comment?"

Joe's words had a strange effect on De La

Rosa because without warning the man lowered his gun and collapsed into a chair.

"Listen," he said in a soft voice filled with urgency. "I didn't steal any money from the foundation. I was the one who was trying to figure out where it was all going!"

"What did you find out?" Frank asked eagerly.

"Well, a lot went to support Jim Ebersol," De La Rosa admitted. "I told Jim he couldn't go on living the way he had been. His last book had disappointing sales, and his TV show had been canceled. But he refused to cut down on his expenses. Did you see the house they rented here? Three thousand a week!"

"So that explains the missing funds?" Joe suggested.

"Some of them, but not all," De La Rosa said, shaking his head. "Even accounting for what they spent, there should have been a lot left over. Either Ebersol was giving it away in bunches without telling anyone, or somebody was stealing from the fund. There's so little left that I had to tell Michele she couldn't have the advance she wanted. That's what we were fighting about this morning."

"What advance?" Frank asked. "For what purpose?"

"She said she was going to take her husband's place and that she wanted to make a big publicity push for herself. She was scary. I mean, the guy was just murdered!

"Anyway, I told her I couldn't sell enough stock from the Ebersol Foundation's trust fund to advance her the amount she needed. There are bylaws that prohibit spending the trust's capital beyond a certain point. And we've already reached that point. She blew a gasket when I told her. She threatened me with everything from murder to firing to a lawsuit. But if you want to know the truth, I think *she's* the one who's been stealing the money. Oh, sure, they both blamed me from the beginning. But it's not my fault, and nobody's going to make it my fault!"

"Stay calm, Mr. De La Rosa," Frank advised. "We're not accusing you of anything."

"How long has money been disappearing from the trust?" Frank asked.

"About a year," De La Rosa said. "Since just after I came on board. Several hundred thousand dollars is what we're talking about. It's put the foundation in serious financial trouble."

"Tell me how the foundation is set up," Frank said.

"Basically, Ebersol is—was—allowed to seek funding from the corporate sponsors of his TV show. The corporations would donate cash or stock to the foundation, and in return he would plug their message and their products on the show. Of course, that all fell apart when the show was canceled."

De La Rosa sighed in frustration. "I kept telling Jim that he had to reestablish his scientific credibility—spend less time on the talk show circuit and more time in the lab, working. And I'll bet in addition to everything else, she's even accusing me of his murder—am I right?"

"No, sir," Frank said, wondering what had made De La Rosa bring that up. "She didn't say anything like that. Only that you belonged in jail."

"Besides," Joe broke in, "they've already arrested someone for Ebersol's murder. Why would she accuse you?"

"I, er, I didn't say that she did for certain." De La Rosa backtracked. "I was only guessing—"

"Tell us more about Ebersol and Michele," Frank urged. "What were they like as people?"

"That's easy," De La Rosa said. "They were two spoiled children who expected everything to be handed to them on a silver platter. They had no idea what anything cost. They just charged everything to the lab and expected money to appear in front of them."

"Is that how she behaved this morning?" Frank asked. "When she demanded the advance from you?"

"Yes," De La Rosa said, frowning. "You know, I don't know why she should care so much about an advance when in a few days she's going to collect a life insurance payment for Ebersol's death."

"Wait a minute," Joe said. "Are you implying that Michele had something to do with her husband's murder?"

"I'm not accusing anyone of anything," the foundation manager said nervously. "Listen, I need to be alone for a while." He walked over to the door and opened it. "Please leave."

"If you want to talk, we're staying right here in the hotel," Frank told him on their way out. De La Rosa nodded, but said nothing more, and closed the door firmly behind them.

"I don't know what to make of that guy," Joe said as the boys walked down the one flight outdoors to the second floor. "He's completely nuts! I thought he was going to kill us!"

"Calm down, Joe," Frank cautioned him. "You're fine, and we just learned a whole lot."

"I guess you're right," Joe said, smoothing his shirt. "So where are we now?" he asked, leaning against the railing that overlooked the street.

"At this point we've got a few suspects in Ebersol's murder," Frank said. "Michele, De La Rosa, MacLaughlin, and Wheeler. But of those four, only Wheeler and Michele had obvious motives, and they had the best opportunity to kill him, too. De La Rosa was in an airplane—at least as far as we know. As for MacLaughlin, he was with us in the tent when the murder happened."

"De La Rosa has a possible motive," Joe pointed out. "If Ebersol knew he was stealing from the foundation, De La Rosa might have wanted to shut him up. We have to check on his flight. Come to think of it, we should check in with Everett, too. He's probably at the observatory."

"I don't think so," Frank said. "I see his van in the lot over there."

The Hardys found Everett in his room, surrounded by papers and charts, a pencil in his hand. Sheets of data from the eclipse were spread out all over the bed and floor.

"There was too much commotion at the observatory, with the police and all, so I brought my data back here," he told them. "The only time I've been out was for breakfast this morning to show Michele the data from my sensors. This is spectacular stuff! From the preliminary results, I'd say we have convincing proof of the exploded planet!"

"That's fantastic, Everett," Joe said, slapping the research assistant on the back.

"If only Dr. Ebersol were here to see this," MacLaughlin said with a sigh.

When Joe and Frank told him about the theft of their film from the tent, MacLaughlin was aghast. "This is a disaster," he said. "We need that film to corroborate my findings!"

"We did manage to save the roll of film that was still in the camera," Joe told him consolingly. "We might get a few good pictures yet."

"Have you developed it?" MacLaughlin asked.

"No," Frank said. "It's in the refrigerator in our hotel room. So far, we've been too busy."

"Too busy?" MacLaughlin said, his face flushing. "Which do you think Ebersol would have wanted you to investigate—his murder or the existence of a possible tenth planet? It's science that matters, not whether any one scientist lives or dies!"

"Take it easy, Mr. MacLaughlin," Joe said. "We're detectives, remember? We only got invited here because we did a science project."

"I don't care why you think you're here," MacLaughlin said, acting more forceful than the brothers had ever seen him before. "The foundation paid for you to come here, and you're responsible for certain things. I'm the head of this research project now, and I expect you to be at the observatory first thing tomorrow morning, getting that film developed. I want a report ready for our team meeting at four P.M. Understand?"

Frank and Joe were stunned. Obviously, MacLaughlin didn't know about Michele's plans to drop him from the team and take credit for the discovery herself.

"Yes, sir," Joe said. "We'll be ready."

"Fine," MacLaughlin said, calming down a little. "Now go do something useful. I have important work to do." With that, he dismissed them. Frank and Joe left the room without another word.

"Well," Frank said when they were outside on the stairs again. "I think we've had enough excitement for one day. How about you? Ready for a quick bite and a long swim?"

"Definitely," Joe said. They stopped at a coffee shop for a late lunch and then hopped into their rental car.

"Let's find the most deserted beach we can," Joe said as they drove along the city streets in the hot afternoon sun.

"Hey," Frank said, as he glanced in the rearview mirror, "I think we're being followed. Check out the black sedan behind us."

Joe took a quick glance over his shoulder as Frank made a right, then a left at the next corner. The black sedan was still there. "Oops," Joe said. "I think you're right, Frank. What do you say we give them a run for their money?"

"Good idea," Frank said, gunning the engine. Away they went, with the black sedan burning rubber to keep up with them. Frank tried speeding up, then jamming on the brakes, taking quick rights and lefts, even a U-turn at a not busy intersection. Nothing worked. "Hang on, Joe!" Frank shouted as he made a sharp right onto a side street.

"Frank! Wait!" Joe shouted—too late.

"What is it?" Frank asked.

"You missed the sign back there," Joe informed him, as a high brick wall loomed straight ahead of them. "It said DEAD END."

Chapter

9

FRANK SLAMMED on the brakes, and the convertible fishtailed to a stop inches from the brick wall. No sooner had the brothers started to breathe normally again than the black sedan turned into the alley, blocking the only exit.

Frank and Joe slid low in their seats, not knowing what they were about to face. Then they heard the voice of Captain Kanekahana shouting to them.

"What do you two think you're doing?" he raged, walking over to them as they stood up and got out of their car. "I ought to throw you both in jail for leading me on a chase like that. Somebody could have been killed!"

"Well, sir," Joe said, trying not to explode,

"if we'd known you were the police, we might not have tried to lose you."

Kanekahana, flanked by two burly men in uniform, gave Joe a withering look. "All right, I'll let it go this time," he grumbled. "But while I've got you here, let me warn you again—this is no game. I got a call from Michele Ebersol, who told me how she'd taken a sedative and fallen asleep on a surfboard. She said you came along and saved her. Now I know you're skilled detectives—but this murder investigation is dangerous. I want you out of this show *now*—understand?"

With that, he got into the car with his men and backed out. Frank and Joe stood there for a little while, waiting to cool down. "I can't stand that guy," Joe remarked as they got back into the convertible and backed out of the alley.

"I'm not too fond of him myself," Frank said.

"Well, there's just one thing to do," Joe said, a sly smile lighting up his face. "Let's catch the killer and present him—or her—to Captain Kanekahana."

"Gift wrapped and tied with a bow," Frank said, nodding his agreement.

The next morning, after showers and a huge breakfast, the brothers took the film canister out of their refrigerator and drove up the mountain to the observatory.

There were a surprising number of people still there. Some were taking down their tents and packing their equipment, while others were using the observatory's extensive facilities to process their data or develop and analyze their film. In the hallway that led to the observatory's darkroom, a crowd of scientists stood waiting their turns.

"It's good we got here early," Frank said. "As it is, we're likely to be on this mountaintop all day."

"Oh, well," Joe said, "we have to meet MacLaughlin here at four o'clock anyway. I figure we'll be just about done by then. I brought two packs of gum. Do you want one?" he asked, pulling out the gum.

The scientists just behind them were arguing their conclusions about the data they'd gleaned from the eclipse. Most of the talk was over the Hardys' heads, but when the subject turned to Ebersol's exploded planet theory, they listened closely.

"I'd like to know if Ebersol found the ring of planetary debris he was looking for," said a tall, middle-aged woman in a lab coat. "How ironic it would be—his greatest discovery, and he didn't live to see the proof."

"I'd hardly call it *his* discovery, even though

he was playing it for all it's worth," said a young man who Joe thought was about thirty.

"You're right about that. I guess he needed something new because his TV show was canceled," a woman wearing khaki shorts and a T-shirt added.

"As far as I'm concerned, the real work on the exploded planet theory was done by MacLaughlin," the man said.

This caught Joe up short, and he could tell Frank was equally surprised to hear this.

"Well, I suppose you could say that," the woman in the lab coat agreed. "But I'm not talking about the donkey work, all the figuring and calculations—I mean the really creative work, the actual theorizing."

"I know that," the young man shot back. "And I'm telling you, it's been Everett MacLaughlin all along. If you read the theoretical papers carefully, you can see the hallmarks of his style. Go back and read his Ph.D. thesis and you'll agree with me. It's as clear as day. Ebersol is—or *was*, I should say—a media star, not a brilliant theorist. He just knew how to steal the show—and the credit."

"Maybe it was more of a symbiotic relationship," the woman in shorts suggested. "Ebersol needed MacLaughlin's tenacity and determination, and MacLaughlin needed Ebersol's salesmanship."

Frank and Joe had refrained from saying anything, not wanting to stop this very revealing conversation. But now it was their turn to enter the darkroom. As they turned the temperature down to chill the room so their film wouldn't be spoiled and got the developing chemicals ready, they discussed what they'd just heard. The air conditioner roared to life then, and it became so noisy that the boys could barely hear each other speak, even though they were shouting.

"Do you believe what they said about MacLaughlin?" Joe shouted to Frank.

"I don't know what to believe anymore," Frank confessed, speaking right into Joe's ear. "Everyone's got a different story. Most people seem to agree that Michele is ruthless and ambitious, and we know she plans to cut out MacLaughlin and De La Rosa. But could she really have stabbed her husband while she was calmly talking to us over the intercom?"

"On the other hand, how could she have missed seeing the killer go into the tent?" Joe wondered.

"Easy," Frank said. "She was staring up at the sky the whole time, not at what was happening on the ground."

"I guess you're right," Joe said, shutting off the lights before taking the infrared film out of its protective canister. Frank flipped the switch that turned on the red light outside, indicating that there was exposed film inside and not to open the darkroom door.

"Ready to go?" he asked Joe as he carefully felt his way along the table to the first tray of chemical wash.

"Ready," Joe said.

Before Joe could unscrew the top of the protective thermos, there was a loud blast from somewhere outside—loud enough to be heard even over the noise of the air conditioner.

"What was that?" Joe said in the darkness.

"Sounded like an explosion," Frank said.

At that moment the door to the darkroom flew open, and something was tossed inside. Something that exploded into blinding blue-white light!

"A magnesium flare!" Frank shouted, covering his eyes.

"Yeow!" Joe yelled, reacting to the sharp pain in his eyes from the sudden exposure to light. He was seized by a sudden coughing fit. Frank, too, was coughing from the fumes.

Joe went out the door into the hallway. The blinding light had burned itself out and the smoke was thinning a little, although the acrid smell of magnesium oxide still filled the air.

As Joe stood in the hallway, catching his breath, Frank came barreling out of the room.

"It was lucky I hadn't opened the film canister when that flare was thrown in," Joe told his brother.

"Not as lucky as you think, Joe," Frank said. "The canister is gone. Somebody stole our last roll of film!"

Chapter

10

Joe felt the blood drain from his face. "No!" he shouted. "Come on, Frank, we've got to get it back!" Without waiting to see if Frank was following him, Joe ran down the smoky hallway to the exit. Pushing it open, he found himself staring at the back of someone.

"What was that explosion?" Joe asked him as Frank joined them. "Did someone set off a bomb?"

The man turned around, and Joe's eyes widened when he saw who it was.

"Tim Wheeler!" Joe cried. "What are you doing here?"

"I'm working on my documentary, remember?" Wheeler told them. "I can't drop my work just because the police think I'm a murderer. Anyway, come with me, I want to show you something."

Motioning to the Hardys to follow, Wheeler led them to the front of the observatory, where he pointed to the parking lot. A vehicle that looked as if it must once have been a van was burning furiously. What little paint remained indicated that the van had been blue.

"Frank," Joe said breathlessly, "that could be Everett MacLaughlin's van!"

"I was just thinking that," Frank replied, biting his lip.

Surrounding the burning car at a safe distance was a crowd of people, watching in horrified fascination. Joe and Frank silently turned to Wheeler.

"I know what you're going to ask, and you're not going to like the answer. I was in the men's room when this happened. So I was all alone. Sorry, but it happens to be the truth."

"Did you see anyone running from the scene or out of the building?" Joe asked. "Because we just had a canister of film stolen from us— from right under our noses."

Wheeler shook his head. "Nope."

"I hate to think about the possibility of MacLaughlin being in that van," Frank said, looking worried.

"I know," Tim said somberly. "And I know

this looks bad for me, too. The police will probably arrest me again when they find out I was up here. But what should I do? Make up an alibi?"

From the direction of the access road, they heard sirens screaming. Wheeler listened for a moment, then picked up the briefcase that was on the ground next to him and said, "I think it's time for me to leave."

Giving them a nod and a tense smile, he opened the driver side door of a nearby car. Then he climbed in and drove away, passing the first fire engine on its way up.

"You know what?" Frank said to Joe. "I really don't think that guy is guilty."

"You don't?" Joe asked, surprised.

"Nope. I think someone's trying to make him look that way. Come on, Joe. Let's see what we can find out."

The Hardys ran over toward the burning vehicle. A group of assistants had been valiantly battling the blaze, without success. Now they were giving way to the professional fire fighters. Joe tapped the shoulder of one young man who was catching his breath. "Do you know if anyone was in the van?" he asked.

The young man shook his head. "It's impossible to tell."

"What exactly happened?" Frank asked.

"I was in the lecture room when I heard a

tremendous explosion," the young man explained. "We all ran out of the building to see what had happened."

Joe nodded to Frank, who must have been thinking what he was. The explosion could have been one of two things—either a bomb intended to kill the driver of the van, or a diversion to get everyone out of the building. That would have cleared the way for the bomber to toss the magnesium flare to steal their film.

The fire engines had all arrived by this time, and right behind them came the police, first among them Captain Kanekahana. He was steaming.

"What in the world happened here?" he demanded. Walking right up to one of the young assistants, he shouted, "Raymond, I thought you were assigned to stay close to Wheeler. What do you think you're doing? And where is Wheeler?"

This particular assistant had obviously been an undercover officer, Joe realized.

"I was trying to help put out this fire, Chief," Raymond began. "The explosion was huge."

"I know it was huge," Kanekahana said, his teeth gritted. "We heard it all the way over in Kailua! What I'm asking you is, what about Wheeler? Where is he?"

Raymond acted very guilty. "Well, Chief, he was in the lecture room with us, along with his film crew. They were shooting part of Dr. Rickhower's lecture on variations in sunspot activity. But then Wheeler left the room, and I tried to follow him, but I lost him. Then the explosion happened, and I came outside to help."

"Let me make sure I heard you right. You 'came outside to help'?" Kanekahana repeated derisively. When the young officer nodded, the captain stormed away, shaking his head in disgust.

"Do you think there were explosives involved?" Joe asked the young man, wanting to be sure. "Maybe the van just caught fire on its own."

"There had to be explosives," Raymond said with certainty. "The fireball was still going when I got out here, and that was twenty seconds after the blast. No way that happened accidentally."

"Wow," Frank said, giving a low whistle.

Joe moved closer to the wreck, with Frank following close behind. Even though the fire was out, Joe could feel intense heat as it continued to smolder. A fire fighter was poking around in the mess and came up with what looked like a charred circuit board in his gloved hand.

"This didn't come from the van's circuitry," he said to a colleague nearby. "No way."

"Excuse me," Frank asked them. "Was anyone in the van?"

One of the men answered simply, "We're not sure yet."

"Anybody who *was* in that thing when it blew would be in a million charred pieces," the other man said solemnly.

Joe heaved a deep breath and turned to his brother. "I hope MacLaughlin wasn't in there. But if he wasn't, where is he now?"

"We have a murder suspect under our nose and we lose him!" Captain Kanekahana's voice bellowed across the parking lot as he stood talking to an officer. "I ought to fire that kid, Raymond!"

"Do you think we ought to tell him what we know about Wheeler?" Frank asked Joe.

"I guess we have to," Joe said. "We probably should have told him about seeing him in our room the other night."

"Captain," Frank said, walking up to him with Joe beside him, "Wheeler drove down the mountain just as you were coming up."

"He did?" Kanekahana's eyes widened, and he pressed a button on his hand-held walkie-talkie immediately. "Car twenty, car twenty, this is Kanekahana, do you read me?" There was a static-filled response, after which the

98

captain said, "Suspect coming down from observatory. Seal both ends of Saddle Road, over."

After receiving the ten-four indicating that car twenty had understood, Kanekahana turned to face the Hardys again. "I suppose you're going to tell me you were here doing research."

"That's right," Frank said. "We found one roll of our film that hadn't been stolen, so we brought it here to develop. When we were inside the darkroom, someone threw a magnesium flare in, and by the time we recovered from the light and smoke, that film was gone, too."

"We suspect the firebomb might have been just a diversion," Joe added.

"Is that so?" Kanekahana said skeptically, then turned to a nearby fire fighter. "Any sign of a body in the wreckage?"

"Not yet, sir," he said. "It's going to be a while."

Kanekahana got on his radio again. "Calling in, car forty-six. What is suspect's status?"

"She's still at the beach house," came the response. "Everything's under control, over."

Kanekahana nodded, satisfied, and signed off. "Somebody, at least, is on the ball," he muttered. "And we won't let Wheeler get off so easy this time."

"Honestly, Captain, I don't think Wheeler's your man," Frank piped up.

"What?" Kanekahana said, startled by Frank's boldness. "You just said he took off down the mountain right after the explosion!"

"I would have done the same thing if I'd been him," Frank ventured. "After all, he's in a lot of trouble already."

"You can say that again," the captain agreed. "And he's going to be in a lot more."

"If you'd just give us a chance," Joe volunteered, "I'm sure Frank and I can clear Wheeler's name."

"You want to clear Wheeler's name?" Kanekahana said, his face getting red. "Isn't that sweet of you."

The captain turned to his men, pointing at Frank and Joe. "I've had enough of these two," he said with a scowl. "They're in the way of our investigation. Besides which, if they don't leave Hawaii in one piece, I'm going to hear about it all the way from the mainland. I've decided to take them into protective custody. Put cuffs on them and take them to a nice, comfortable cell downtown—and keep them there!"

Chapter

11

"WAIT A MINUTE! You can't arrest us!" Joe shouted, his anger rising. "We haven't done anything!"

"I'm not arresting you," Kanekahana said with an annoying smile. "I'm just placing you in protective custody. You did say there have been attempts on your lives lately, didn't you?"

"We can take care of ourselves," Joe insisted. "We haven't asked for protection, and we don't want any."

"That may be true," Kanekahana said patiently. "But as far as I'm concerned, you two have caused me all the trouble you're going to. I want you both out of harm's way and out of my hair. I can't think of a better way to do that than to put you away for a day or two, behind bars, where you'll be safe and sound. Take them away, men," he said, smiling.

Before Frank or Joe could say anything more, they were herded into the backseat of a waiting patrol car.

For the next hour or so, the boys waited in the steaming hot sedan, drenched in their own sweat, as Kanekahana questioned those who had witnessed the post-explosion fire. The captain seemed in no hurry to do anything with the Hardys. In fact, on the few occasions when Frank or Joe complained to one of the officers, they were told to sit tight. The officer then went to check with someone higher up. In each case, nothing was done for the brothers.

Finally, when Kanekahana was finished, he slid into the front passenger seat. Ignoring the Hardys, the captain turned to the driver and said, "Hey, it's sweltering in here. Turn on the air conditioner."

Soon the air conditioner was blowing cool air over the Hardys, but Joe's and Frank's tempers were flaring hotter than ever.

As the driver guided the patrol car slowly down the mountain road, Frank addressed the back of Kanekahana's head, trying his best to be polite. "Captain, one person in this case is already dead," he said. "Maybe two—if

MacLaughlin was in that van when it went up. Someone's tried to kill us, and maybe Michele Ebersol, too. Don't you think we'd all better work together to solve this case? It won't do any good to lock us up."

"This case is no mystery to me," Kaneka-hana answered coolly over his shoulder. "Tim Wheeler had the means, opportunity, and motive to murder Dr. Ebersol. He should have been kept in jail after Ebersol's murder, but unfortunately, I had to go along with the court and let him out on bail. Now he may have committed a second murder. So this time, when we catch him, he's going to stay caught no matter what. And when this is all over, I'm going to call for a review of our local judge— I'd like to see her head handed to her on a platter!"

"But, Captain," Joe said, making an effort to sound calm, "Wheeler couldn't have been behind the attempts on our lives. And as for our stolen film—"

"Save your breath. We've already gone over all this," Kanekahana snapped.

"But don't you see?" Frank broke in. "The car bomb was probably a diversion! It was a way to get everyone out of the building while the perpetrator threw the magnesium flare to ruin our film!"

Kanekahana's derisive laugh sent a chill up

Frank's spine. "I've got to hand it to you boys," he said. "You sure do have active imaginations. What makes you think you're so important or that your film is at the center of this case? You were just photographing the eclipse, after all."

"I don't know," Frank said. "But if we want to get to the bottom of this, that's what we've got to find out."

"All right, then," Kanekahana said, facing them with a triumphant smile. "When we bring Wheeler in, you can talk to him about it yourselves—with an officer present, of course."

A short time later, after the squad car had passed the police roadblock on Saddle Road and reached Kailua, the driver pulled up in front of police headquarters. The Hardys were escorted to a small holding cell, where their cuffs were not removed. The cell door was slammed on them, and the Hardys were alone in the cell. "Do you believe this?" Joe said to his brother. "They're treating us like criminals!"

"He sure is," Frank agreed. "I'll tell you what I think, Joe. Kanekahana wants to nail Wheeler for Ebersol's murder, whether he's guilty or not. I guess he's more interested in advancing his career than in seeing the real murderer put to justice."

"Well, we can't let him get away with it,"

Joe said hotly. "I agree with you now. Wheeler's not guilty, Frank—but De La Rosa may be. I wish we could check his arrival time from the mainland. That would tell us a lot."

"All it would take is a phone call," Frank said, a gleam coming into his eyes. He reached into his pants pocket and pulled something out.

"What's that?" Joe asked, noticing the small, pointed object.

"My trusty lock pick," Frank replied with a grin. "Don't leave home without it."

"Are you sure we should use it in here?" Joe asked nervously.

"You're the one who said we're not criminals. We haven't even been charged with anything," Frank pointed out. "We're only in jail under protective custody, and I bet any judge would agree we can take care of ourselves."

Joe nodded slowly and held up his handcuffs for Frank to unlock. Soon they were both free. Frank then unlocked the door of their cell. In no time they were in the hallway. Before moving on, though, Frank clipped both pairs of cuffs to their cell door. "A little present for Captain Kanekahana," he said with a tight grin.

"Where to now?" Joe asked, glancing nervously up and down the empty corridor. Their guard could return at any moment, and Joe wasn't eager to be caught there.

"To a pay phone," Frank informed him, heading toward the door at the end of the hallway. "Got some change?" Joe gave him a handful as they slipped through the door and up a flight of stairs.

Moments later the Hardys were at a pay phone near the men's room. Officers occasionally passed by, but none of them recognized the Hardys, and there was nothing to indicate that the brothers were escaped prisoners. Trying to act nonchalant, Frank dialed Information. Moments later, he dropped a coin into the phone and dialed the number of a ticket agent.

It took about ten minutes, and talking to several different agents, for Frank to learn that Richard De La Rosa had not arrived in Hawaii the night after the eclipse. Instead, he had come on the same flight as Tim Wheeler!

"So it seems the Ebersol Foundation's manager has no alibi after all," Frank told his brother, hanging up from the last call.

"Wait till we tell Kanekahana about this!" Joe said jubilantly. "For all we know, he doesn't even know about De La Rosa."

"I'll bet he does, Joe," Frank told him. "He's spoken to Michele, remember?"

Forgetting that they were supposed to be locked up in a holding cell, the boys raced downstairs. In the lobby they ran smack into

Kanekahana, whose jaw dropped when he saw them.

Frank and Joe told the police captain what they'd found out. Instead of reacting excitedly, Kanekahana nodded grimly and said, "I already know all about that." Glancing down at their wrists, he said, "I see you've been a couple of busy bees."

Instead of reprimanding them for escaping, Kanekahana merely sighed. "Oh, well. It doesn't matter now. Come with me, boys. There's something I think you ought to see. In fact, I was just coming down to fetch you."

Without another word, he led the Hardys to his squad car. The Hardys climbed inside, and Kanekahana drove them out of the parking lot and down the main street of Kailua.

"Where are we going?" Joe asked from the backseat. The captain didn't respond. In silence, he turned right down a main avenue, then left down a side street, and finally pulled into a dead-end street very much like the one where he'd cornered the Hardys earlier. At the head of the street were two squad cars, their blue and red lights flashing.

Under a palm tree, in front of a run-down bungalow, Joe spotted a small blue car with rental plates. "Have a look inside," Kanekahana said.

The Hardys got out of the squad car and

walked over to the sedan. There in the front seat, with the thermos containing their last roll of film on the seat beside him, was Richard De La Rosa. His mouth and eyes were open, and a look of frozen terror filled his face. A gun lay in his limp hand.

"A dead man is not a pretty sight, is it?" Kanekahana muttered. "Not a pretty sight at all."

Chapter

12

DUMBSTRUCK, Joe turned to Frank, then to Kanekahana. "It looks like a clear-cut case of suicide," the captain said, handing Joe a note in a plastic evidence envelope. "We found this on the seat beside him. There weren't any prints on it except his. I think it makes everything pretty clear."

Joe read the note out loud. " 'I stole the money from the foundation. Michele kept accusing me of it, and I always denied it. Then last week she told Ebersol, and he started threatening to prosecute me. I had to kill him—there was no other way. I tried to kill Michele, too. I would have succeeded if those two kids hadn't interfered.

" 'It's all over for me now. I deserve what I got. I don't ask for forgiveness, but I hope those I have hurt will forgive me anyway. R. De La Rosa.' "

The entire note was typed, including the name, Joe noticed.

"I know what you're thinking," Kanekahana said. "Why didn't he sign it? I've been asking myself the same question. But I think the answer is that there's no telling how an agitated person's going to act. Or maybe there was no pen or pencil around."

"Or maybe he didn't write the note," Frank said levelly. "Maybe someone wrote it for him. I'm surprised that didn't occur to you, Captain. Especially since Tim Wheeler is still missing."

"Wrong," Kanekahana said heavily. "My men picked Wheeler up coming down Saddle Road after he fled from the observatory. He's been freed already because of this note.

"Look, you two," he added, meeting the Hardys' gazes squarely. "I admit I was wrong about Wheeler. I guess my own wishful thinking clouded my judgment. And I apologize for taking you in. Consider yourselves free to come and go as you please. This case is closed."

"Wait a minute, Captain!" Joe broke in. "How can you be sure this is a suicide? I agree that Wheeler didn't kill Ebersol, but you can't be sure De La Rosa did, either. What if Michele or someone else killed De La Rosa and planted this note? Remember, De La Rosa was the manager of a foundation. He would know enough about legal matters to realize that a typed signature isn't very convincing."

The captain took the note back from Joe, a look of sheer irritation on his face. "I said I was sorry for hauling you in. Don't make me do it again, okay? Just go on back to your hotel and let me take care of things."

"But what about Joe's point?" Frank persisted. "It's entirely possible that Michele Ebersol could have murdered De La Rosa."

"Wrong! She couldn't have," Kanekahana said triumphantly. "My men were watching her all day, and she never left her beach house. I only called off the surveillance after we found De La Rosa's body."

"Are you sure it was wise to call off your men so soon, Captain?" Frank asked.

"Don't forget about MacLaughlin, either," Joe pointed out. "He's been missing all day, hasn't he? His van got fried at the observatory, but where is he?"

"Maybe blown to bits," Kanekahana said. "In any case, he couldn't have killed Ebersol. By your own testimony, he was in your tent with you when the murder was committed." He held out both hands to indicate that the point was obvious and that the conversation was over.

"By the way," he said, changing the subject, "can you two get back to your hotel on your own? Or do you need a lift?"

"It's not far. We can walk," Joe answered. "We'd like to stick around for a while, though, just in case you come up with some new information."

"I doubt that will happen," the captain said with a shrug. "But you're welcome to stay. I realize I've been wrong about you. I hope there are no hard feelings?"

Having been proven wrong, Kanekahana, Joe realized, was now trying to make amends to keep from getting in trouble for the way he'd treated them.

"Captain," Frank said, "we'll let it all go, no problem. But on one condition. You've got to at least consider the possibility that De La Rosa didn't kill himself."

Kanekahana opened his mouth to respond, but before he could say anything, another officer came up to him.

"No prints on that thermos, Captain," the officer said. "Should we open it now, or do you want to take it back to the bomb squad?"

"Bomb squad?" Frank repeated. "No, that's our infrared film in there!"

"What's so important about a roll of film?

That's what I'd like to know!" Kanekahana exploded.

"I have no idea," Frank admitted. "But De La Rosa—or whoever's behind all this—must have thought it was important, or he wouldn't have gone to such trouble to steal it."

"Hey!" Joe said, snapping his fingers. "I just remembered something. MacLaughlin was going to meet us at the observatory at four o'clock. If he's alive, he might be there for our meeting."

Kanekahana checked his watch. "It's twenty of four now," he said. "Tell you what. I'd like to see what's on that film of yours. I'll make you a deal—I'll drive you up to the observatory, and we'll keep a guard on you while you develop the film. Then you hand it over to me as potential evidence."

Joe and Frank looked at each other. "Does this mean we're back on the case?" Frank asked. "With your approval?"

"What case?" Kanekahana sighed, and the corners of his mouth turned up ever so slightly. "As far as I'm concerned, this case is just about closed. We're just tying up some minor loose ends. Now let's get going."

MacLaughlin never showed up for the four o'clock meeting. It took about an hour for the Hardys to get the darkroom set up and refrigerated. The staff at the observatory were very cooperative, especially when they saw the police escort that had come with the Hardys.

After another hour the film was developed and ready. Frank and Joe stood in the darkroom with the lights on, examining their handiwork.

The photos were about one inch by one inch, and had yet to be enlarged. For now, they were on contact sheets, which Frank held up to the light. Each frame had a small clock face in the lower left-hand corner to indicate the precise time the photograph was taken. Thirty-three of the thirty-five pictures had been shot over a space of fifty seconds.

"Gee," Joe said sadly. "It makes you realize how much of our stuff is still missing. How many rolls did we take? Nine?"

"Yup," Frank answered, sighing. "These are great, though. And look—could that be the ring of debris we were hoping to find?"

Joe squinted his eyes to get a better look. There, in the bottom third of the photo, was a faint blur that looked something like the rings around the planet Saturn. "That could be it," Joe said eagerly. "It's hard to tell until we enlarge it."

"Wait a minute," Frank said, peering intently at the top left picture, the very first one taken. "What happened here?"

Joe scrutinized the photo. The image was marred by what was a radiating semicircle that filled the bottom half of the picture. "What's that?" he asked.

"Beats me," Frank replied. "Let's enlarge it."

The enlargement process took them another few minutes. To Joe's surprise, the shot was neither a double exposure nor a flaw in the film. "That's someone's head!" he cried. "I must have shot this picture by accident while I was handing the camera over to you."

"Can *you* make out who it is?" Frank asked.

Joe took a closer look, but because this was an infrared photograph, a picture of the heat emanating from objects, not of the objects themselves, it was impossible to tell who might have entered the tent. "You'd think we'd have heard someone entering the tent," Joe remarked.

"Not if they didn't want us to," Frank said. "Remember, it was pitch-dark, and the air conditioners were making quite a racket."

"What do you say we show these to Kaneka-hana?" Joe asked. "Much as I hate to turn any evidence over to that guy, we did promise."

Frank nodded. "But first, let's enlarge the

rest of these. Maybe we'll find something else important."

When they had finished, the boys had thirty-two clear views of the sun, many showing the ring of debris Ebersol had predicted would be there. "Wait till MacLaughlin sees these!" Joe enthused. Then he realized something. "If he's still alive, that is."

"They sure do look convincing," Frank said, gathering them up. "But except for this first one, they don't help us with Ebersol's murder. Let's go show Kanekahana what we've got."

The captain was impressed with the accidental photo and asked Joe to explain how it was taken. "I loaded one camera while Frank shot the eclipse with the other," Joe explained. "When his roll was empty, he handed his camera to me to reload, and I handed him the fully loaded one."

"I see," said Kanekahana. "Now why would someone have come into your tent in the middle of the eclipse?" he asked. "And what does that have to do with Ebersol's murder?"

Before anyone could answer, an officer sprinted up to them. "Captain!" he said, breathing hard. "We just got a call from the emergency room at Kailua Hospital. They found MacLaughlin!"

Chapter

13

"THEY FOUND MacLaughlin?" Kanekahana repeated. "Then he's alive?"

"He's alive, but he's pretty banged up," the man answered. "According to the nurse who called the station house, he's suffering from scratches and bruises, plus some confusion and dizziness."

"All right, let's get down there." Turning to the Hardys, he said, "You two can go back to your hotel now, or take a swim, or whatever. I'm going to head over to the hospital. I promise we'll take good care of these photographs."

"Hold it, Captain," Joe insisted. "We're coming with you."

"We want to see MacLaughlin," Frank added.

"The man's in the hospital," Kanekahana said. "It's bad enough I'm going to have to interview him. If you want to talk to him, it can wait till morning."

"We want to know where he's been, and what happened to him," Joe said. "It may have a lot to tell us about the explosion up there at the observatory. De La Rosa didn't mention the explosion in his suicide note, remember?"

The captain looked them over and shook his head. "Oh, all right," he said with a reluctant smile. "I suppose as long as I'm there, you'll be able to stay out of trouble. Why don't you take your own car, though, and follow me down there."

"That's right," Frank said. "I forgot our car was still here. We'll see you at the hospital, Captain. Come on, Joe."

Frank and Joe raced for their car and followed the squad car down to Kailua Hospital. On the way they passed the busy Kailua strip, which was full of tourists sampling the various clubs, restaurants, and shops. Joe wished he could check some of them out instead of checking out the hospital, but a pleasure trip to Hawaii would have to wait for another time.

MacLaughlin was in one of the examination rooms just off the emergency room. He was sitting up on the gurney, staring at his ankles, when Frank, Joe, and Kanekahana entered with the attending physician.

"He was scratched up pretty badly when he got here," the doctor told them. "He didn't even know who he was when he wandered in. We had to identify him from his driver's license. We're going to keep him overnight for observation, but you can have a few minutes with him in private before we move him upstairs." With that, the doctor left the room.

"All right, Mr. MacLaughlin," Kanekahana began, standing over his bed, "suppose you start from the beginning and tell us just what happened this afternoon."

"I—I drove up to the observatory earlier today," MacLaughlin said in a weak voice. "I had work to do. but on my way into the building I was waylaid by Tim Wheeler—"

"Wheeler?" Kanekahana said to Joe and Frank with a raised eyebrow.

"No, it's not what you think," MacLaughlin stopped him. "He just wanted to interview me. Well, I said yes, and we went off to an empty room at the observatory. Afterward he left, and I went to the parking lot to get some notes that I'd forgotten in the van. I was a few feet from it, when there was this enormous blast. It lifted me right up into the air, and the next thing I knew I was lying in a thorn bush on the side of the mountain. I guess I was thrown over the railing of the parking lot. But I didn't know that at the time. I didn't even know who or where I was for a while."

"Someone blew your van up," Kanekahana volunteered. "You were lucky they set the radio-controlled bomb off a few seconds too early. They were probably anxious and pressed the button before they meant to."

"What happened then?" Frank asked Mac-Laughlin.

"Well, I felt kind of dizzy and lost, like I said, and I just started walking downhill. I realize now, of course, that I should have gone back up to the observatory. I just kept walking and walking. I didn't even feel my cuts until I saw the blood on my clothes. I made it down to the main road, and some guy in a truck picked me up and gave me a lift into town. He dropped me off outside the hospital. I guess I passed out at that point because the next thing I knew, I was in this bed."

"Mr. MacLaughlin," Kanekahana said, "I have some bad news for you. Richard De La Rosa shot himself today."

MacLaughlin's eyes widened, and he sat up slowly. "He's dead?"

Kanekahana nodded. "Suicide. He left a note saying he'd killed Dr. Ebersol. Apparently, he'd been stealing from the foundation. He admitted that, too."

MacLaughlin was truly stunned. "Michele," he whispered. "Did he mention her?"

"Michele?" Kanekahana echoed. "Why, no. What makes you ask?"

MacLaughlin was staring into space, nodding his head slowly. "I'll bet Michele drove him to it," he muttered. "Maybe she even killed him and made it look like suicide."

"What?" Joe asked.

"I'll bet she killed him like she killed Dr. Ebersol," MacLaughlin added quietly.

"You're saying Michele Ebersol killed her husband?" Frank asked.

"She *and* De La Rosa," MacLaughlin said. "They were in it together, I'm sure of it. Now she's gotten rid of her partner, too. She's probably on a plane to Australia."

Kanekahana stared hard at the assistant. "Mr. MacLaughlin," he said, "what makes you think De La Rosa and Michele Ebersol conspired to murder her husband?"

"Because," MacLaughlin said, "they conspired in everything! They were both stealing from Dr. Ebersol's foundation. They were in love, too! They wanted to get rid of Ebersol so they could have the profits from his work and the foundation's money. Michele has always wanted the foundation as her own. She plans to take credit for the exploded planet discovery, but none of it was her work. Not that that would stop her. And now that she's gotten rid of her husband and her partner, she'll probably come after me, too."

MacLaughlin's eyes widened in fear as the revelation seemed to dawn on him. "The car bomb! She must have set it! Captain, you've got to arrest her!"

As Frank listened, a number of thoughts floated through his mind. He remembered how Michele had vowed to be rid of MacLaughlin, and what the scientists had said about the exploded planet theory being Everett MacLaughlin's work.

"But if they were in love, why would she kill De La Rosa?" Kanekahana asked MacLaughlin. "His death showed every sign of being a suicide."

"Michele doesn't like to share," MacLaughlin told him. "Without De La Rosa she'd have it all, I guess—the foundation, the money, the fame. She ordered me to bring her the videotapes of the eclipse recorded by my detectors. She told me that if I didn't give them to her, she'd cut me out of any new grants and ruin my career." He turned to the Hardys, an urgent tone in his voice. "Maybe you two can stop her. Please don't let her destroy what Dr. Ebersol worked so hard to create!"

The captain turned to his men and said, "Don't let this guy out of your sight. Come on, you two," he added to the Hardys. "We're going to check in on Michele Ebersol."

They were out of the hospital in no time, and racing in a caravan along the coastal highway, with the captain's siren screaming.

"Do you think there could be anything to what MacLaughlin said?" Joe asked Frank as they raced to keep up with the police car ahead of them.

"It's possible, I guess," Frank said with a shrug. "There's definitely a lot more to Michele Ebersol than meets the eye. But I don't see how she could have set off that car bomb or killed De La Rosa. She was under police guard all day. Right?"

"We'll soon find out," Joe said. "Anyway, maybe she just drove De La Rosa to do what he did. You know? I mean, maybe she had some kind of hypnotic influence over him. It's been known to happen when a guy really falls for a woman."

"The last time we saw De La Rosa," Frank commented, "he seemed more afraid of Michele than in love with her."

"Well, maybe by that time she'd turned on him," Joe offered.

"Or he on her," Frank said. "Remember, she was the one passed out on the surfboard, not him."

Just then they arrived at the beach house.

An ambulance, sending off circular beams of red light, sat in the driveway.

"Now maybe Kanekahana will believe this case isn't over yet," Joe muttered as Frank pulled over and parked. The brothers both stared at the front door of the beach house, where paramedics were coming through carrying a stretcher.

Lying on the stretcher was the motionless Michele Ebersol.

The Hardy brothers got out of the car and hurried over. "What's going on?" Joe asked one of the paramedics walking beside the stretcher, holding a plastic container of intravenous fluid.

"Looks like an overdose of sleeping pills," the paramedic told them.

"Is she going to be all right?" Frank asked.

The medics had reached the back of the ambulance and began hoisting the stretcher up. "We're going to try electric paddles and a stomach pump," said the one who'd answered them first, a grim expression on his face. "But I'm not getting my hopes up. I think we got here a little too late. She has no pulse—no pulse at all."

Chapter

14

THERE WAS no time to get Michele Ebersol to the hospital. The paramedics set to work trying to revive her in the back of the ambulance. They used electrified paddles to shock her back to life. A third medic began setting up a stomach pump.

Kanekahana was furious, barking curses at everyone around him, but Frank knew the captain had to be the angriest with himself. If he hadn't taken the guard off Michele after De La Rosa's body was found, this wouldn't have happened.

"Where did you find her?" the captain asked the paramedic who was setting up the pump.

"Out by the pool," the young man answered. "There was an empty bottle of sleeping pills on the ground beside her. Looks like she meant to do away with herself."

Kanekahana kicked a nearby ambulance tire and spat out a few grumbled words. "Did she leave a note?" he asked.

"Not that we saw," the paramedic said.

"I'd better go check," Kanekahana said, marching into the house. Frank and Joe hesitated, reluctant to leave Michele Ebersol while her life hung in the balance.

"There's nothing you can do for her," the paramedic with the pump said to them. "If we can save her, we will. Go on inside if you want."

Frank nodded to Joe, and they hurried through the front door. Inside, Frank spotted two videocassettes on the living room floor in front of the VCR. "These are MacLaughlin's tapes, the ones she ordered him to bring to her," Frank said, reading the labels. "She must have watched them."

Joe walked over and picked up the tapes. "We're going to hold on to these for dear life," he said. "They're not going to disappear the way our film did."

Kanekahana entered the room from the french doors that led out to the veranda. "No note," he said. "Still, it does look like suicide."

"MacLaughlin claims Michele murdered De

La Rosa," Frank pointed out. "But how could Michele have gotten away from the police who were watching her long enough to kill De La Rosa, and—"

"Forget it," Kanekahana said. "There's no way! Not while my men were still here. The guy's just raving. The explosion must have rattled his brains."

"Wheeler managed to give your guys the slip," Joe said. "Why not Michele?"

Frank could tell from the flush that colored his face that Kanekahana didn't like hearing that.

"Joe, I think the captain's right," Frank pointed out in an effort to smooth the captain's ruffled feathers. "Michele's been watched carefully almost since her husband's murder. It would have been pretty hard for her to steal our film, push herself out to sea, set off that car bomb, kill De La Rosa, then come back here and kill herself!"

"That's right, wise guy," Kanekahana snapped at Joe. "There's no suicide note, but that doesn't mean much. She might have been in cahoots with De La Rosa. Maybe De La Rosa meant to protect her by taking the rap himself. Or maybe she tried to kill herself because she was so upset over her husband's death. Or maybe over De La Rosa's, if he was her partner. Or if one of my officers mentioned his death to her as they were leaving . . .''

He let out a sigh and shook his head. "I guess there are some things we'll never know—unless Mrs. Ebersol recovers, that is. If she dies, I'm going to have to close the case. I think we've gone as far as we can."

"Not quite, Captain," Frank said. "We still have that floating image of a head on our photograph taken during the eclipse. Maybe when we blow it up, it might reveal something more. And maybe—just maybe—Michele Ebersol will pull through and be able to tell us something."

"Let's go see how she's doing," Joe suggested, and the three of them went back out front. The paramedics seemed to be excited, and one of them came right over to Kanekahana.

"It looks like she's going to make it," he said, wiping the sweat from his brow. "I've got to hand it to you, Captain. If you hadn't sent your men out here to find her, she'd have been dead for sure. She took a lot of pills."

Kanekahana smiled for the first time that Frank could remember. "I had a funny feeling something might be brewing," he said. "In this business you learn to trust your instincts. That's what I was just telling these two kids here."

Frank had to smile at the captain's bravado, while Joe, who was standing behind the captain, rolled his eyes and grinned.

When the ambulance sped away into the night, its lights flashing, the captain turned to the Hardys and said, "That about wraps it up for now. You can find your own way back, can't you?"

"Sure, Captain," Joe said. "But if you don't mind, we'd like to have a look at MacLaughlin's tapes of the eclipse first."

"Well, if you're going to do that, maybe I'll watch, too," Kanekahana said. "Not that I think they'll have anything new in them, but you never know."

They all went back into the house and Frank flicked the TV on to Channel 3.

"Here we go," Joe said, pushing the tape into the VCR. Soon, they were staring open-mouthed at the incredible video of the solar eclipse. There in full-color, computer-reconstituted images was the black circle, surrounded by a series of flares rising up from its surface. Above and behind the flares, Frank and the others saw a faint series of specks—the planetary debris that Dr. James Ebersol had predicted would be there. Proof positive that another planet had once existed!

"There's the exploded planet Dr. Ebersol

was looking for!" Joe said, his eyes riveted to the screen. "Too bad he didn't live to see it."

Frank and Joe clapped each other on the back excitedly, but Captain Kanekahana seemed only mildly impressed. "Well, I'd better be going," he said, getting up and making for the door. "I need my sleep if I'm going to tie up this investigation properly. See you tomorrow."

When Kanekahana was gone, Frank reached for the remote and rewound the videotape. "Let's watch it again, Joe," he said. "It's just so incredible."

They watched it again, and then again. It was about two-thirds of the way through the third viewing when Frank noticed something he hadn't seen before. Something amazing. Something that, if he wasn't mistaken, would prove who the murderer was.

Grabbing the remote again, he rewound the tape thirty seconds back and played the key section again. No, he hadn't been mistaken. There was the proof they'd been looking for, right before his eyes. "Do you see what I see, Joe?" he asked.

"I'm not sure," Joe confessed. "Play it again."

This time, Frank wound the tape all the way back and played it the whole way through.

When they reached the key section, Frank said, "Now watch here."

Joe paid close attention, and Frank watched his brother's eyes light up at what he saw. "I don't believe it!" Joe gasped. "It was MacLaughlin—and we can nail him with this, Frank!"

"Not quite," Frank cautioned his brother. "The videotape is only circumstantial evidence. We'd have to search MacLaughlin's room to see if we can find solid evidence to back up our theory."

"Right," Joe said, reaching over and ejecting the videocassette. "Let's get out of here."

They got in their car and headed in the direction of their hotel. "He'll be at the hospital tonight, so we can do a good, thorough search of his room," Frank said, smiling as he leaned back in his seat and gripped the steering wheel tightly.

"I still don't get it, Frank," Joe said. "How could one person possibly have committed all those crimes?"

"I have to admit, it sounds improbable that anyone could have pulled it all off," Frank said, "but MacLaughlin could have if anyone could. Think about it, Joe. He was on stage with Ebersol when he nearly got fried. He was up on the mountain when someone tried to run us down. He was at Michele's the morning she wound up on that surfboard, and he was up at the observatory when his van blew. I know he claims he walked down the mountainside after the car bomb went off, but what if he didn't? What if he had another car stowed? He could have driven down to town, shot De La Rosa, then gone to Michele Ebersol's and drugged her before heading straight to the emergency room."

Joe screwed up his face. "There are two problems with that theory. One, MacLaughlin was in the tent with us during the eclipse. How could he have killed Ebersol? And the second question is why? Why would he do it?"

"That's something we'll have to learn from MacLaughlin himself, or maybe from Michele," Frank said, pulling into the hotel parking lot. "We really are lucky Kanekahana sent his men out there when he did. As for how MacLaughlin could have killed Ebersol—well, you've got that video in your hands, Joe. Put it together with that photograph with the unidentified head. Think about it—you tell me how he did it."

Joe thought for a moment, then nodded slowly. "I see what you're getting at," he said, gripping the videocassette a little bit tighter.

The brothers got out of the car and hurried up to MacLaughlin's room. Fortunately, there was no one in the hallway. As Joe stood watch, Frank removed the lock pick from his wallet and used it on the door. It creaked open, and they crept inside.

The place was dark and close. Clearly, MacLaughlin must have told the hotel staff not to clean his room. "I'll check out the bedroom, Joe," Frank whispered. "You look here in the sitting room."

Joe nodded and tiptoed straight ahead into the stifling darkness. Frank stepped forward and then to his left, entering the bedroom.

"Nobody home, Frank," Joe said, entering the room and flicking on the light. "Whoa! This guy is a slob!"

MacLaughlin's bedroom was a housekeeper's nightmare. Clothes and papers were scattered everywhere. "It almost looks like somebody's ransacked the place," Frank commented. "It wasn't nearly this bad last time we were in here."

"Well, if you're right, and MacLaughlin's our man, he certainly wouldn't have had time to clean up."

"And maybe that will be his downfall," Frank said, a smile creeping over his face. "Let's have a look around, Joe. What do you want to bet we find something?"

Looking around the room, it was clear that MacLaughlin's life was lived primarily in a lab. Everywhere Frank looked he saw half-written formulas, scrawled notes and drawings, dog-eared books, and scientific journals.

"Nothing much here," Joe said, disappointed.

Frank dropped to his knees, checking under the bed and dresser, and said, "Not so fast, Joe. I think I may have found something."

Getting up, Frank braced himself against the dresser. "Help me push it away from the wall," he said.

Joe came over to help. Soon they had edged the heavy piece of furniture far enough from the wall so that Frank could reach behind it. He felt his hand brush against cloth, and moments later he brought it out and held it up.

Both their faces tightened at the grisly sight. In his hand, Frank held the piece of damning evidence they needed. It was a plain white shirt—except for one thing. The front was smeared with a large, dark red streak of blood!

Chapter

15

"THIS IS IT, Joe," Frank said, gulping hard. "We've got the proof we need!"

"Unless someone planted it to make Mac-Laughlin look guilty," Joe pointed out.

"Hmmm—that's always a possibility," Frank admitted. He checked out the room until he spotted a discarded plastic dry cleaner's bag. Carefully wrapping the bloody shirt inside the bag, he unzipped the small pack he wore around his waist and placed the bag inside the pack. "I don't think it's a plant, though," he added. "Not when you consider that videotape and the photograph with a head. What we need now is a confession from MacLaughlin. Then Kanekahana could really nail him."

135

"How can we get a confession?" Joe wondered.

"I think I have a way," Frank said mysteriously. "After we do some work on the video, we'll get some sleep. Tomorrow morning, we'll invite Captain Kanekahana to join us on a visit to MacLaughlin in the hospital, and we'll bring these videotapes along, too."

The moment Joe's head hit the pillow, he was out like a light. It seemed just moments later that Frank was calling his name, urging him to get up and get dressed.

Frank made a quick call to Captain Kanekahana, asking him to make sure MacLaughlin wasn't released from the hospital early, and to meet them there. The brothers grabbed a couple of muffins and some cans of juice, got in their car, and pulled out onto the Kailua strip.

"It's too early for traffic, I guess," Joe said, staring at the empty road.

Frank gripped the wheel and gazed straight ahead, but he seemed lost in thought. "Joe," he said after a few moments, "remember the jacket MacLaughlin was wearing in the tent during the eclipse? He must have used it to cover his bloody shirt after he stabbed Dr. Ebersol."

"You mean he sneaked out of our tent while we were concentrating on the eclipse, took off the jacket, went to Ebersol's tent, stabbed him, came back, put the jacket back on, and went back to work?" Joe said with a shiver. "That's a pretty grisly scenario. But you know something?" Joe realized suddenly. "It really explains how that ghostly head got on our film! I must have snapped a picture without realizing it when I handed you the camera, so that picture must be MacLaughlin's head as he was sneaking back."

"Right," Frank agreed. "The timing works, Joe. Think about it. He comes back into the tent as you snap that picture. Then he finds that his videotape has jammed, or broken, or overheated while he was gone. So later, when he has the time, he makes a copy of the video, using the first two and a half minutes of the tape twice—at the beginning and then again at the end—to cover the part of the tape that was lost!"

"It makes perfect sense," Joe said. "And the timing of the photo I took would fit right in with that scenario."

"Come to think of it," Frank said, "MacLaughlin never took off his jacket after the murder. He was sitting there the whole time, wearing it!"

"He had the bloody shirt on under it during the first interrogation," Joe realized, grimacing at the thought. "Why didn't he just get rid of it?" he asked as Frank pulled onto the avenue that led to Kailua Hospital. "It would've been easy to stuff it in any trash container in Kailua."

"The shirt might have been found and traced back to him," Frank pointed out. "From the time of the murder on, remember, MacLaughlin was incredibly busy. He was probably waiting for a free moment to get rid of the shirt once and for all. Only that moment never came."

"But why would he kill Ebersol, Frank?" Joe demanded. "MacLaughlin obviously loved his work. Why would he kill the man who gave him his greatest opportunities?"

"We'll have to find that out from Mac-Laughlin," Frank said as they pulled into the hospital's parking lot.

Joe could see Kanekahana pacing in front of the entrance, waiting for them.

"Well, you two, I have some interesting news," he said, smiling broadly as Joe and Frank strode toward him. "It turns out that Michele Ebersol was in cahoots with De La Rosa after all."

"What?" Joe and Frank shouted in unison.

"You were right, Joe," Kanekahana said, smiling. "She must have given my guys the slip at some point yesterday afternoon."

"But, Captain," Frank said, almost shouting, "MacLaughlin's your murderer, not Michele!"

"I've got proof of Michele's guilt," Kanekahana assured them. "Rock-solid proof."

"But we've got proof of MacLaughlin's guilt!" Joe said, confused.

Kanekahana waved his hand dismissively. "My men found the radio control for a car bomb hidden behind a dresser at her house," he told them. "Her fingerprints are on it. Add to that the fact that she was the one with the best opportunity to kill her husband and I think you'll see—just as any jury will see— that Michele—"

"Wait, Captain," Frank said. "If you'll just let us show you our evidence, you might change your mind."

The captain shook his head. "Go ahead," he said with a shrug. "I'm listening."

"Let's start with this then." Joe handed the stunned captain the bloody shirt they'd found.

"And when you're done with that," Frank added, "we've got a videotape to show you. You've seen it before, but I think you'll be surprised at a little something we all missed the first time around."

A few minutes later Frank was pacing restlessly as Joe and an officer fumbled with wires and cables, setting up the VCR they'd brought to MacLaughlin's hospital room. MacLaughlin, who was dressed and ready to leave the hospital at noon, sat on the edge of his bed, looking uncomfortable.

"I see you're better this morning, Mr. MacLaughlin," the captain said cheerfully. "The doctor says you're fit as a fiddle and ready to leave."

"Which is just what I'd like to do now," MacLaughlin replied nervously. "I don't see why you're in such a hurry to look at my videotape, or even why you're here, Captain."

"Oh, I'm very interested in science," the captain replied. "Let's get started, shall we? Ready with that tape, Joe?"

Joe popped in the tape and flicked on the TV.

"Here we are at the beginning of the eclipse," Frank said as the startling images came on. "You sure did a great job of programming the computer image enhancement, Mr. MacLaughlin. There's no doubt at all about the ring of debris."

"I always knew it would be there," MacLaughlin said, staring at his work.

"Joe and I were fooling around last night and intercut our roll of photos with your last two and a half minutes of video," Frank said. "I think you'll be interested in this. Each of our photos has a time marker, as you can see."

Everyone in the room was silent as the tape ran, but Frank noticed that MacLaughlin was growing more and more fidgety.

The darkened sun on the last part of the videotape began to be interrupted by the images the Hardys had taken. The eclipsed sun was remarkably similar on the photos, and yet, subtly different from the videotaped images. Frank wondered if MacLaughlin had guessed yet what they were up to with their little demonstration.

"Well, there's the proof," Frank said at one point, staring at the image of a ring wrapping around the eclipsed sun. "Proof that there was once another planet in our solar system."

"I'm a bit of a novice at this," Kanekahana said, sitting down next to MacLaughlin on the bed. "Would you mind explaining it to me, Mr. MacLaughlin?"

"Be happy to," MacLaughlin said. "You see, for years the evidence was there for anyone who cared to look—the subtle irregularities in the orbits of the other planets that made no sense unless there had once been another planet among them. It's like a dance with many performers when one of the dancers is missing. The clues are there, but it takes a careful, unbiased observer to realize that someone is no longer there."

"Fascinating," Kanekahana said. "Go on.

I'm intrigued by all this—evidence, subtle ir-regularities, clues—it all sounds a lot like what we do down at homicide."

MacLaughlin snorted. "I guess you could say that, on some crude level, there is a connection. At any rate, imagine what tremendous stress the tenth planet must have been under for it to be ripped apart like that! It was literally torn apart by the sun's gravitational pull."

MacLaughlin continued even after the tape had stopped playing and Joe shut off the VCR. His speech was full of passion, yet clear, Frank realized, listening intently. In fact, MacLaughlin's explanation was much clearer than Dr. Ebersol's had been. Listening, it was obvious to Frank who had first come up with the exploded planet theory. And yet, Ebersol had claimed it entirely for himself. How angry would that have made MacLaughlin?

Angry enough to kill, Frank answered himself. "Everett," he said, "if you're so clear about all this, then why doesn't your videotape of the last part of the eclipse match our photographs, taken at the very same time through a connection to the very same telescope? Does that disprove your theory? Will you have to wait for the next eclipse to be sure?"

Frank's words had the intended effect. MacLaughlin's face drained of all color, and he began to tremble. "The differences you're pointing out are trivial," he snapped. "I noticed them, of course, but they could be due to any number of factors—inferior photographic equipment, for instance, or mistakes in the developing process!"

"I don't think so," Frank said tenaciously. "I think you forged the last two and a half minutes of your videotape. Joe, pop in the second tape and let Mr. MacLaughlin see what I mean."

Joe did as he was asked. MacLaughlin sat frozen on the bed, intense hatred crossing his face. The second tape was the same as the first, except that the scene was split. The images of the eclipse were the same on both sides of the screen.

"There, you see?" Frank said, pointing at the screen. "On the left is your videotape of the *first* two and a half minutes of the eclipse. On the right is your video of the *last* two and a half minutes. Watch the flares. See how they happen at exactly the same time? I'm afraid there's no doubt about it, Everett. You've doctored your videotape. That kind of tampering may seriously spoil your case for the existence of the exploded planet."

"No, it won't," MacLaughlin insisted. "Maybe I did doctor the tape, but I only did it because the equipment overheated during the final minutes of the eclipse. The last part of my videotape was ruined, so I duped the beginning and ran it onto the end of the tape. That doesn't change the fact that I've got four and a half minutes of the real thing—which is more than enough to prove my theory!"

"Your theory?" Frank interjected. "I thought it was Dr. Ebersol's theory."

"I— Of course it was his," MacLaughlin mumbled, reddening again. "I only meant that I—"

"But I know the *reason* your equipment overheated, Mr. MacLaughlin," Joe stepped in to say, just as the image on the TV screen changed to show the ghostly head from the Hardys' accidental photograph. "It's because you weren't there to tend to it! You were in the tent next door, getting your final revenge on your mentor for stealing your ideas and claiming them as his own!"

Kanekahana turned to face the speechless MacLaughlin. "You may as well give up now, Mr. MacLaughlin," he said calmly. "We have a bloodstained shirt of yours, and I'm sure you know whose blood it is."

Horrified, MacLaughlin fell back onto the bed, his hands covering his face as a sob erupted from his throat. The captain laid a comforting hand on his shoulder. "At least it's over," he said. "You won't have to lie anymore."

There was silence for a moment as Mac-Laughlin tried to control himself. Then, in a sudden movement that caught them all by surprise, he reached over and pulled Kanekahana's gun from the holster at his waist.

"Wrong, you idiots," the scientist growled, jabbing the weapon into the police captain's side. "It's not over yet—not by a long shot!"

Chapter

16

"PUT YOUR HANDS on top of your heads and don't make a move—any of you!" MacLaughlin cried, his eyes darting around the room. "If anyone tries anything funny, the captain will take a bullet in the heart."

"What do you hope to prove?" Frank said, forcing down the urge to attack at once. "You can't get away with Ebersol's murder—not now."

"I've gotten away with it so far, haven't I?" MacLaughlin bragged. "Now I'll have a police captain to ensure my safety."

"You'll never make it, Everett," Joe said, clasping his hands on top of his head as he'd been ordered to.

"What do I care?" MacLaughlin asked. "My life is ruined already. I've got nothing left to lose." He let out a bitter laugh. "For years I was Ebersol's devoted servant—his faceless, loyal assistant. And what did I get for it? Nothing! Once he married that showgirl who had the nerve to call herself a scientist, he forgot about me. I found myself taking orders from her! Before I knew it she was taking over the foundation, plotting to run it herself when he retired. She wanted me out from the very start, and she wasn't subtle about it either."

MacLaughlin was breathing hard as the story poured out of him, releasing all the pent-up anger that had already resulted in the deaths of two people and threatened the life of a third.

"When I first came to Ebersol with the exploded planet theory, he acted as though I was crazy," MacLaughlin went on, jabbing the gun into Kanekahana's side so hard that the captain winced in pain. "He laughed at me. Laughed in my face! But a week later, I heard him presenting the theory to the rest of our team as his own!

"And everyone loved it. They loved the glamour of it, the mystery, the magnitude. I didn't say a word. Who would have believed me, anyway, if I'd said the theory was mine?

"Michele and De La Rosa encouraged him

to make the theory public. They thought it would turn his floundering career around. They started planning—the exploded planet book and the exploded planet documentary. They were even talking to bigwigs at a theme park about getting an exploded planet attraction! All Ebersol needed was the proof this eclipse was going to give him.

"And through all of it, did I get a thank-you? No! What I got was the feeling that Michele and De La Rosa wanted me out, and Ebersol was going along with them."

"So you made them both pay," Kanekahana said coolly. "You killed Richard De La Rosa, didn't you?"

"I didn't plan on killing him," MacLaughlin said. "I just wanted to make him see that putting Michele in charge of the foundation was a big mistake. He pulled a gun on me, and I panicked. We struggled, and before I knew it, he was dead."

The regret on MacLaughlin's face quickly vanished. "But I'm not sorry," he said coldly. "He deserved to die. They both did. That's why I went back last night to see her. I was determined to finish her off once and for all. I thought leaving the bomb remote there was inspired. It would prove that Michele and De La Rosa were in cahoots to kill Ebersol. That's why I made up the story about their being in love. I guess you saw through that little ruse. Well, nobody's perfect. After all, I'm a professional scientist. As a killer, I'm only a beginner."

"Michele Ebersol is alive, in case you hadn't heard," Kanekahana interrupted. "She'll be our star witness against you when your case comes to trial, Mr. MacLaughlin."

"My case will never come to trial," MacLaughlin said. "Because I'm getting out of here! Come on, Captain, we're going to walk out of this room now. I'll be right behind you with this gun aimed at your back. It'll be under the jacket I'm folding over my arm. So don't try anything funny. You two, stay right where you are or the captain dies, understand?"

Kanekahana had no choice but to do as the man said. As he stood, Frank cried, "Wait! Before you make your escape, you've got to tell us something—how did you do it all? What you managed to accomplish in such a short amount of time was amazing!"

"You were lucky in a thousand ways," MacLaughlin said bitterly. "You were lucky I didn't manage to run you down that first morning on the hill. You were lucky my equipment overheated during the eclipse. You were lucky you didn't die when I tripped you on the side of the mountain and that you hadn't opened your film canister when I threw the magnesium flare into the darkroom. Need I go on?"

"All right, we've been lucky," Frank said, thinking fast. "But you were going to tell us how you killed Ebersol."

"I knew I would be just as brilliant at murder as I was at astrophysics," MacLaughlin bragged. "Once I made my decision, I vowed to persist until I was successful—just as any good scientist does. I started out by rigging the podium at the university, so his electrocution would look like an accident. If you hadn't knocked him away the way you did," he said to Joe, "it would have been all over then.

"Once we got to Hawaii, I tried to get rid of you so you wouldn't be able to get in my way. But when that didn't work, I persisted. I left the tent when the eclipse was at its height, when every last person on that mountain was looking at the sky, not at me.

"He never knew what hit him. He just looked at me, surprised that I was there. I didn't want to use a gun because of the noise, so I stabbed him, quick. I knew there wasn't any time to spare. I had to get back into the aluminized tent before the eclipse was over."

"What about Michele Ebersol?" Frank asked. "You went to see her the next morning. But that wasn't when you drugged her, because she still saw De La Rosa."

"Right," MacLaughlin said. "After I left, I doubled back. I watched her argue with De La Rosa over the foundation's money like two vultures fighting over their prey. I sneaked out to the pool patio and slipped the drug into the iced tea she'd left there when they started arguing. After he left, she went back out and finished it. When she was out cold, I carried her to the beach and laid her on the surfboard. Bad luck again that you two showed up in time to save her."

"What about the car bomb?" Frank asked.

"I rigged that as a diversion," MacLaughlin bragged, "so that I could expose your film with the magnesium flare, or at least steal it. I should have destroyed it once I got it, of course," he said regretfully. "That was a mistake. But when I killed De La Rosa and went back to my room to write the suicide note, I decided that leaving the film with him would make the note more believable."

"Very clever," Kanekahana said, sounding impressed.

"After that, I had only one person left to deal with—Michele. I went to her house and dropped off the videotapes. Oh, I was good. I acted very stoic when she told me she was firing me from the team. But before I left, I slipped another dose into her iced tea. Then when she was weaker, I went back in and forced the bottle of pills down her rotten little throat."

"After that, you headed for the hospital?" Kanekahana asked.

"Not before I'd run through some torn bushes to mess myself up a bit," MacLaughlin answered. "Then I walked out to the road and waited for someone to drive by and take pity on a poor, wandering soul. You've got to admit, for a first-timer, I did make a brilliant murderer."

"You certainly did," Kanekahana said. "But why add another crime to the list? Things will go much easier with you if you just give yourself up now."

"Are you kidding?" MacLaughlin said, laughing mirthlessly. "If I give myself up, I'll never see the light of day again! No thanks. I'm going to disappear to someplace the law will never find me, and I'm taking you with me, Captain. Now let's clear out of here!"

Until then MacLaughlin hadn't relaxed his vigilance for a moment. There'd been no opportunity for Frank and Joe to make a move. Then just as MacLaughlin began to move, nudging the captain ahead of him, an unexpected thing happened. There was a knock at the door.

"Mr. MacLaughlin?" came a familiar voice from outside. "It's me, Tim Wheeler. I was wondering if we could do that interview you promised. Is this a good time?"

In a moment of stunned silence as MacLaughlin hesitated, not sure what to do, Joe quickly jerked backward and spun around, dropping to his knees at the same time. With one swift motion, he balled his hand into a fist and sent it crashing into MacLaughlin's kidney.

The gun went off with a loud bang, but it was no longer pointed at Kanekahana. Across the room, the TV screen shattered from the bullet's impact. Before MacLaughlin could get off another shot, Frank had pinned the arm with the gun to the floor and landed a left hook to MacLaughlin's jaw that made his eyes roll back in his head.

Kanekahana leaped over the corner of the bed, grabbed his gun, and pointed it at the now unconscious MacLaughlin's right temple. "Send some men up to MacLaughlin's room right away," he said into the walkie-talkie that was clipped to his belt. "You should have stuck to science, my brilliant friend," he added to MacLaughlin. "Your career in crime is over."

"Whew, that's some story," Chet said, giving a little shudder before poking the last bite of his candy bar into his mouth. "That guy MacLaughlin sounds like a real sicko."

"He sounds pathetic to me," Biff said. Chet and Biff were back in the Hardys' bedroom, where once again Frank and Joe were getting dressed for a special occasion.

"By the way, where are your suntans, guys?" Chet asked, frowning. "You look like you spent the whole time indoors."

"We didn't exactly get a chance to go surfing," Joe said regretfully, knotting his tie. "We'll have to do that next time. Right, Frank?"

"You're on," Frank replied. "I guess MacLaughlin felt ignored and underappreciated for years," he said. "It must have driven him over the edge. We were lucky we decided to watch his tape more than once."

"Not just lucky," Joe countered. "A little talent went into the mix, too."

Frank sighed, blowing on his knuckles and rubbing them up and down on his lapel. "Yes, it's true. I cannot tell a lie. I'm talented, and Joe's lucky."

Biff and Chet let out a laugh, and even Joe had to chuckle. Just then Laura Hardy's voice came wafting up the stairs. "Are you boys planning to go to the Astronomy Club tonight?" she called. "Your father's holding my seat. Come on, get a move on!"

"You heard her," Joe told his brother. "Duty calls."

"Right," Frank said, nodding. "Biff, Chet— it's time to go. We've got a little presentation to make about the exploded planet."

"Yeah," Biff said, grinning as he threw an arm around each Hardy brother. "And you're the 'stars' of the show!"

Frank and Joe's next mission

When Fenton Hardy, the father of detectives Frank and Joe, sets off to Seattle on a case of his own he has no idea it will end with him being accused of murder and kidnapped before he can clear his name. His sons are soon on hand to pick up the trail where their father left off. From the death of a university professor to the mysterious quarantining of a small Washington town, the brothers follow a trail of lies and deceit that finally leads them right to their father's door and into the middle of a deadly doomsday experiment.